DIG TWO GRAVES

DIG TWO GRAVES
A NOIR THRILLER OF REVENGE

ANDREW HALLMAN

Copyright © 2025 by Andrew Hallman

All rights reserved.

No part of this book may be reproduced in any form or by any electronic or mechanical means, including information storage and retrieval systems, without written permission from the author, except for the use of brief quotations in a book review.

*For Daniel and Traci,
with gratitude for your
enduring friendship
and generous support*

CHAPTER ONE

IS THERE anything more humiliating than clomping along Tamiami Trail in the clothes you wore into the joint four years before? Oversized Gucci hoodie, already making him sweat. Old school Jordans, more battered than he remembered. DKNY acid-washed jean shorts he has to hitch up with nearly every step to keep from falling down around his ankles—skinny after four years of that jail slop. To all the people gawking at him from their cars it must look like he's clutching his nuts.

The hell you gawking at? Like you ain't never seen a person walking on the sidewalk. That's what it's here for. For shitheads like me, who don't have a whip.

Who don't even have a belt.

So what if you look like a homeless man, he tells himself. *You friggin ARE a homeless man, bro. Don't make you any less of a man.*

Except it DOES, of course. Don't get it twisted.

That's the way the world works. The world ain't tryna hear your sob story. The world just wants to see if you got money or not, if you in the game or not, and the world ain't got time to spare you but a glance. They know the deal just from seeing you walking.

But this shit is temporary.

Hard to walk home, when you ain't got a home to walk to. Especially on a March morning, the sun already blazing down on you like the Lord's righteous fury. Of course he'd thought a lot about what he was going to do once he was out, but somehow he hadn't really given much consideration to this actual moment, to these first steps. He'd seen it all playing out starting from the moment he came into the yard, at the house that used to be his home. Tara, his daughter, squeals and charges at him—four years ago, she'd just taken her first wobbly steps—and he gets down on his knees like the sinner he knows he is and gives her the biggest hug ever. Shelly's maybe standing in the doorway looking on, trying hard not to smile.

The back-stabbing, monkey-branching cunt.

Could he have gotten them to meet him at the courthouse, and give him a ride? Yeah, probably.

Well—

Maybe.

He rode the bus down from Charlotte County with nothing but a check for fifty dollars in his pocket, which then cost him seven to cash. When the bus reached its stop and he stood up, he recognized a guy at the front who was getting off in Naples as well—they'd both worked in the kitchen for a bit. Billy? Jimmy? Something vanilla like that. Short white guy who actually played basketball in the yard.

He'd watched Billy step down from the bus into the sunlight, blinking, hesitant, like a groundhog after hibernation. Watched as an enormous woman ran up to him, threw her arms around him, greeting this loser like she'd won something.

He stepped down from the bus, slid past the reunited

couple. Thought about wishing Billy luck—except he wasn't sure that was actually his name. Thought about asking for a ride.

Instead, he started walking. Knowing it would take all morning, and then some.

Mandalay Villas is little more than a glorified mobile home park, a warren of single-story two-bed-two-bath bungalows that barely survived Ian and got slammed again by Milton. So he heard, anyway. He draws a few stares, a hesitant wave, as he walks along the unnecessarily weaving road, designed to keep drivers from going above the posted fifteen mph speed limit. Which he appreciates, now that he has a daughter who would be one of the "children at play," as the sign says. That is, if her mother allows her out to play. Which he doubts.

"Hey, Von." It's Sherman, the neighborhood narc, purring up alongside him on his four-wheeled scooter. "You're back. Good to see you."

"Sherm," he says. He does not slow down, does not stop, does not reach out a hand. "You got a new scooter."

"Had this baby a couple years now," Sherman says. "New to you, I suppose."

Von nods, keeps walking. "Been a while."

"When'd you get out?"

"Today, Sherm."

"Today?" Sherman's scooter hums as it matches Von's pace. "You walk all the way here?"

The question makes him aware of the dark stains on his hoodie, the damp clinginess of his shorts. Those blisters on his heels. "All the way, Sherm."

"Shelly expecting you?"

"Should be."

"Alvin is there, you know."

Alvin Macalester, the sheriff who sent him up. "Then I guess Shelly's expecting me." He resumes his pace, brushes on past Sherman.

"Just remember, Von—freedom is the most valuable thing any of us have."

He stops. "What about our health?"

Sherman throws his scooter into reverse and turns sharply, pointing himself back toward his house at the development's entrance.

"What about our time, Sherm?" *What about four years of wasted time?*

The scooter lurches away. Sherman calls over his shoulder, "I'd hate to see you go right back in."

Sure you would, he thinks. *There's nothing you'd like better, than to shake your head and tut-tut over my sorry ass.*

But don't you worry. He resumes his course. Just another couple of houses now, one final turn. *I ain't about to give that puppet Alvin another chance. I'm in full control of myself, of my faculties, of my emotions.*

I'm here to see my daughter. I'm here for Tara.

The rest of the world, as far as I am concerned, can fuck right the fuck off.

There is only one vehicle parked in the street: a white SUV, stationed prominently along the curb directly in front of his house, the word "SHERIFF" lettered across the doors in dark green and gold. A waist-high chain-link fence surrounds the patchy yard, and as he lifts the latch to the gate, the front door opens, and Alvin emerges.

No surprise. Also no surprise that Shelly and Darnell remain in hiding. Cowards.

Alvin covers his balding head with his silly cowboy hat. His long cigarette-yellowed mustaches droop along either side of his mouth like he's some marshall from Wild West days. His strap perches up high on his hip, and the butt digs into the expansive sides of his beer belly, which jiggles in his tight-fitting short-sleeved shirt as he totters down the stoop's three steps.

"Von," he says, cheerily. "Glad to see you're out."

"No you're not," Von says, though not very loudly, as he crosses the yard.

Alvin comes to a stop at the foot of the stoop. Strategically. Hands on hips.

"You're looking good."

"No I'm not."

"You seem determined to be contrary today, Von. That's not a good sign."

"I'm just here to see my daughter."

"That can be arranged, of course," the sheriff says. "But you gotta go through proper channels."

"This is my house."

"It's a rental," Alvin says, with a sigh, "and you haven't paid your share of rent since well before I arrested you. This is all ancient history."

"I have a right to see my daughter." Von moves left to sidestep the sheriff's bulk.

A surprisingly firm hand on Von's chest halts him, prevents him from reaching the stoop.

Von looks down at the hand: tan, pudgy, thick-fingered. A class ring and a gold wedding band stand out among surprisingly dark tufts of hair. Alvin has—smartly, correctly—pivoted to block Von with his left hand, swiveling his right hip back out of reach, and covering his strap with his right hand.

"Be smart," Alvin says. "Stand your ground laws are in effect."

"This ain't your property."

"You never know what they might be carrying." He cocks his cowboy hat back toward the front door. "For self-defense."

They.

"So that bitch Darnell's living there now, too?"

"I don't know what the domestic arrangements are," Alvin says, "and I don't care. All I know is if you want to see your daughter, you need to go through proper channels. Unless you want to go back to prison."

Von peers at the sheriff, seeing if he can't establish some sort of man-to-man eye contact through those ridiculous aviator sunglasses. But all he can see in the mirrored surfaces is his own face: doubled, distorted, blue-tinted, bug-eyed.

He steps back into the yard, and Alvin's hand drops down to his side.

"Shelly," he calls, toward the living room's large picture window, glass dark, blinds drawn down behind. Then, louder, "Shelly!"

"There's a right way to do things," Alvin says. "Get yourself a lawyer."

"Get a lawyer," Von scoffs. "Like I'm made of money."

"Well, this is the thing." Alvin steps away from the stoop, toward Von. One more step and he'll be able to sidestep that fat fuck and reach the door with no problem.

The sheriff lowers his voice into the reasonable mumble that Von remembers so well, and hates so much. "You need to establish a residence, get yourself a job. Set yourself up, and then you work through the courts. Of course you have rights —but rights are much easier to exercise when you're legit. When you can prove that you've turned a corner. When you have a place of your own. I'm sure the courts can work out some sort of custody arrangement."

"I ain't talking about custody," Von says to Alvin. Then,

to the opaque glass, "I just want to see Tara! I just want to say hi. Is that asking for so much? To see my daughter?"

People are starting to gather in nearby yards, and in the street behind him, despite the sweltering afternoon heat beating down, browning the remaining patches of grass at his feet. He doesn't know how much further he can push this, before Alvin starts talking about disturbing the peace or some such nonsense.

The door opens behind Alvin, sucking the screen door back into the jamb with a soft bang, startling both of them.

Golden light fills the frame, then is obscured by Darnell's considerable bulk. The backlight burnishes his close-cropped fade into a halo.

"Hey Von," Darnell says, as he pushes open the screen door.

"Hey." Von nods in acknowledgment, but can't bring himself to say the traitor's name. *Judas*, he would have to call him. He'd worked on construction crews with this guy for, what—all his adult life? He was the one who convinced Raul to hire Darnell, when Raul was insisting he didn't want to hire any black guys, saying they didn't work as hard as Mexicans. He was the one who covered for Darnell when his dad got sick. How much flak did he take for this guy? How much shit did he eat for him? How many rounds did he buy for him after they'd put in a shift?

Only for him to stab him in the back. Rat him out to his butt-buddy Alvin. Rip off his girl. And now try to play daddy with *his* daughter.

"Come on in," Darnell says, as he leans out of the house, throwing the screen door wide open.

What?

CHAPTER
TWO

DARNELL RAISES HIS VOICE, and calls to the neighbors. "Hey y'all," he says, that phony Alabama drawl even more pronounced, "Von's back. Come on over, say hi. We got some cake and ice cream."

Cake and ice cream? You fucking with me? What sort of Jedi mind tricks you think you're playing here, son?

Darnell beckons to Von. Alvin is already squeezing in past Darnell, doesn't need to be asked twice.

"Get in outta the heat," Darnell says to Von.

He shrugs, and climbs the once-familiar concrete steps. Brushes the door jamb to avoid touching the traitor, who is taller than him, broader.

More muscly maybe—but not tougher, Von thinks. *Especially not now. I've been working out in the yard.*

He ducks his head as he crosses the threshold, squints as his eyes adjust to the gloom. Alvin stands in the middle of the living room. The sofa and loveseat are new. Pale green leather. Probably fake. Probably rented. His old barcalounger is there, but shifted to the far side of the room. How many evenings had he sat there, feet propped up, beer in hand, yelling at the screen while money he'd bet evaporated before his eyes as yet another coward threw away his pride for the sake of a payday. The shit was always fixed.

Behind him, Darnell is bellowing out his invitation again to the entire friggin neighborhood.

Some of his former neighbors do actually cross the yard and follow him inside. They reach for his hand, shake it. Clap him on the shoulder.

"Nice to see you, Von."

"You're looking good, Von."

"Welcome back, Von."

Not welcome home, mind you. Welcome back.

Turns out some people have no dignity. No pride. Some people will do anything for some free cake and ice cream.

Not that he's going to say no. He's starving. Water first, though. He finds Darnell in the kitchen, cutting the sheet cake —just a plain yellow cake, vanilla frosting. No lettering or anything. As basic as it gets. Two sweaty plastic tubs of store-brand ice cream: one vanilla, one chocolate.

"You got this for me?" Von asks.

"It's your big day," Darnell drawls.

Von senses Alvin behind him, leaning against one side of the double-wide opening that connects the kitchen to the brightly chattering living room on one side, the darkened dining room on the other. Stuffing his face with cake, but keeping an eye on him all the same. Darnell is dressed in baggy gray sweats and a short-sleeved polo that hugs his biceps. His toes spill out over the sides of his contoured sandals, and the pale skin of his soles wraps up the sides of his feet, reaching toward his ankles even.

Darnell cuts him a hunk of cake, then passes the paper plate over the ice-cream tubs.

"What'll it be?"

"I've got a choice, huh?"

"Or one of each," Darnell says. "Up to you."

"Why choose," Von says, locking eyes with his former friend, "when I can just have it all?"

"You got it." The ice cream is already quite soft—the central air is struggling to keep up with the front door being open and the influx of warm bodies. Darnell doesn't bother rinsing the scoop after digging through the chocolate, and leaves a bit of chocolate poop in the vanilla.

He hands Von the plate. Saliva flushes through his mouth.

"Ebony and ivory," Darnell says, with a smile. Then goes so far as to sing, softly: "Live together in perfect harmony."

Where is your pride, man?

Down the darkened hall behind him are the bedrooms. Which door is Shelly hiding behind? Door one, or door two? The master bedroom, that she used to share with him? Or Tara's room?

"You know raising another man's daughter makes you a cuck, right?" Von asks.

Alvin coughs behind him.

Yeah, I know you're standing there, asshole. It's just a question.

"Come on, now, Von," Darnell says, voice soft. Meek.

"That's the dictionary definition," he continues. "Don't know if you're aware of that fact."

"Nobody can replace a girl's father in her life," Darnell says. "You know that."

"But they can rip off a man's girl, no problem."

"Things weren't good between you and Shelly before you—"

"Before I what? Before I was betrayed? Is that what you were going to say?"

"Howbout another slice of that cake?" Alvin, of course. Inserting himself where he isn't wanted.

"You got it." Darnell takes the sheriff's plate and cuts another square from the sheet.

Von takes his cake and ice cream and plastic spoon into the living room, as Sherman pushes through the front door, breathing heavy from the effort of standing.

"Can't keep Sherm away from the sugar, can you?" Von says.

"That's right," Sherman laughs.

Nobody is sitting in his barcalounger, and so he crosses the room to perch on the edge of it. Wanting nothing more than to lean back and kick up the footrest and close his eyes and take a nice long nap and wake up and rub his eyes and say to Shelly, who'd be playing on the floor with their gorgeous little daughter, *Oh man, what a fucked up dream I just had, you wouldn't believe it—I gotta lay off the sweets*. Instead he combines a spoonful of vanilla with a hunk of cake, and lets the cold sugary concoction melt on his tongue, while Alvin and then Darnell file dutifully back into the room, hunting for a place to sit. Alvin perches on the broad arm of one of the sofas; Darnell pulls in a chair from the dining room, and then another one for Sherm.

He's cleaned his plate, he realizes, while the neighbors are politely picking at theirs and making small talk.

"I was always a fast eater," he says. "Even before prison."

His joke gets a few smiles and glances.

"You want some more?" Darnell asks.

"Nah," he says. "I'm good."

Then, as Darnell returns to his conversation with Sherman, he says, "Yeah, actually, now that you're offering, I'll take another round."

"Sure thing," Darnell says. He stands up, sets his own plate down on the chair, crosses the room. Holds out his hand. "Same as before?"

"That'll do," Von says. He has to fight to keep from

smirking and shaking his head in disgust at Darnell's complete lack of self-respect.

But he ain't stupid, Von thinks. *Being all nice and welcoming. Putting me on the spot in front of all these people. To keep things from getting ugly.*

Trying to distract me from my purpose with his bread and circus.

We'll see about that.

Darnell returns from the kitchen with a hunk of cake even bigger than the first, as are his two scoops of ice cream. He nods as he takes it from his ex-friend, then sets it on the coffee table, like he'll get to it later. He only asked for seconds to punk Darnell and make him fetch in front of all his phony friends.

And he's about to ask about Tara when one of the neighborhood old heads, Carmine from a couple doors down, asks him what sort of job prospects he has lined up.

"I've only been out a couple hours," Von says. "I can't just snap my fingers."

"I was wondering if they had any programs to help you make the transition," Carmine says.

"Help?" Von scoffs. "Ain't nobody tryna *help* a guy like me."

"We'd all like to help," Alvin says.

"Okay," Von says, turning his attention back to Darnell. "Howbout getting me my job back with Raul?"

"I wish I could, man," Darnell says.

Oh yeah—the hell you do.

"But I don't work there anymore."

This news takes Von by surprise. "Really?" Darnell had always seemed so grateful for the job that he figured Darnell would eat Raul's shit for the rest of his life, if he could. "You get out of the construction racket?"

"Not entirely. I'm an electrician now."

"Licensed?"

Darnell nods, swallows. "Did some training after hours."

"No shit. I bet that pays pretty good."

Darnell nods. "Not bad."

"You do any work for Raul?"

Darnell cocked his head back, as though thinking about it. *Thinking about what lie he wants to tell*, Von thinks.

"We coincided on one job—but he's exclusively a GC now, he's got his own guys."

"So you never talk to him?"

Darnell shook his head, gave a rueful chuckle. "He never liked me all that much. You thinking about hitting him up?"

"Thinking about it."

"There's building going on everywhere," Sherman says. "What with Ian and Milton."

"We can't catch a break," Carmine says.

"Building and demo," Alvin says. "There are so many new demo companies now, I'm sure they'd be hiring."

"I don't do demo," Von says. "I'm a builder."

"I'm sure you'll find something soon," Alvin says, to a roomful of nodding, cake-eating stooges.

"Look, this is nice and all," Von says. The scoops of ice cream on his plate have deflated into soft mounds, surrounding his untouched cake with a brown and white moat. The sugary mess from the first round has soured in his gut. "I appreciate the concern—I really do. But I ain't here for career counseling. I'm here to see my daughter. It's been four years."

"Shelly brought her to visit," Darnell says.

"Twice. Twice! And that was early on."

"You were the one who told them not to come back," he says.

"You think I want my daughter seeing me in that place?" Von says. "Come on, bro. What sort of an effect is that going to have on a child? How's she gonna respect her father, seeing him like that?"

He feels the hush, in his bones. He looks up, and there she is.

Shelly.

He hates himself for smiling—a reflex. Hates his heart for catching in his throat so he can't even just say hello like a normal person.

She looks skinnier than he remembered. Maybe it's the tortoiseshell-rimmed glasses and her hair cinched up in a loose, wispy knot that are making her cheeks look gaunt. Maybe it's the fine lines at the corners of her mouth, the worry-notch between her carefully plucked and redrawn eyebrows making her look older than he remembered. The lack of makeup.

Wouldn't want to seem to be making an effort for your ex-husband, now would you? For the man you were so sure you could do better than?

And yet here you are, living in the same house, with a clown who used to be your old man's protégé, and you looking like the frumpy housewife you always swore you'd never become.

Still pretty, sure. Maybe he has dodged a bullet, though.

She was always going on about how time affects women more than men. Hell, that's why we had Tara in the first place—

And there she is too, Tara, arms wrapped around Shelly's left thigh. His daughter. Their eyes meet, briefly, and then she mashes her face into Shelly's leggings.

Shelly's legs look skinny to Von. Not anorexic or anything, but she's definitely lost weight.

"Hey," Von says. "Little Tara—look at you. Not so little anymore."

He leans forward, pushes the coffee table back over the shag, which causes a few drinks to lap over their brims and form little quivering puddles on the glass. He gets down on his knees, and opens his arms.

Only for Tara to turn and bury her face in between Shelly's thighs.

She won't even look at me. Neither of them. Shelly despises me, and her hatred has turned my own daughter against me.

"Aw," someone says. "Look who's bashful."

Shelly rolls her eyes heavenward and huffs a sigh.

"It's me," he says, in as calm and comforting a voice as he can manage. "It's... daddy. I'm here now."

Shelly kneels and tries to pry their daughter apart from her legs. She glances in his direction—for the first time—and gives him her "meaningful" glare, the meaning of which he'd never been able to catch, aside from the very vague "DO SOMETHING." Classic Shelly, never wanting to take accountability for anything, always looking to shift the blame to someone else.

He stands, picks his way between the coffee table and misshapen toes protruding from sandals and flip-flops. Squats opposite Shelly and reaches for Tara, who rocks her head violently back and forth, catching her carefully combed-out hair in Shelly's glasses and mouth.

His arms are tiring. He can feel himself starting to flush. The flop sweat starting up again.

Fucking embarrassing. My own daughter hates me.

"It's having all these people here," Von says, with an angry glare at Darnell. *This fucker—he knew what he was doing.* He lowers his arms. "It's throwing her off."

Shelly stands and pushes their daughter toward him.

"Please, girlie," she says. Von detects the undercurrent of exasperation. Shelly's permanent state of being: always fluctuating somewhere between annoyed, irritated, and exasperated. "It's your father."

Von puts a hand on Tara's shoulder and tries to pull her to

him, but this just causes the surprisingly strong girl to lean even harder into her mother, nearly bowling her over. His knuckles press into Shelly's thighs as he tries to extricate his daughter from her mother. When what he ought to be doing —by rights, if not by law—is reaching for Shelly, and hugging her to him, their daughter in between their loving embrace.

In some other world...

"Be good," Shelly huffs. "Just say hi."

"No!" Tara shouts, voice muffled by her mother's thighs.

This brings titters from behind Von.

"She's spirited," one of the old neighbor ladies says.

"Like her momma," another says. "Feisty."

If she gets that from anyone, Von thinks, *it's from me.*

He removes his hands from his daughter. Raises them above his shoulders, palms out. Last thing he needs is some sort of complaint filed. With witnesses ready to sign off on whatever bullshit Sheriff Alvin puts in front of them.

"I know when I'm not wanted," he says over his shoulder, with a chuckle he hopes doesn't sound too forced.

"Do you, though?"

He turns back around like he's been slapped. The meaningful glare again. Though this time it's clear what the SOMETHING is that he should DO: get the fuck out.

Ain't that Shelly for you? In a nutshell. Right in front of everybody—she doesn't care. What a miserable bitch.

She's leaning over Tara, hands on the girl's back, pressing her to her legs now, as though protecting her. Shielding her. When she knows that's absolutely not necessary.

She's trying to press my buttons. That's what all of this raggedy-ass shitshow is about, he realizes. *They're trying to press my buttons, trying to get me to react emotionally. Trying to get me to do something I'll regret later, surrounded by witnesses. By the law.*

But that was the old me. This is the new me.

They don't know the new Von.

"I'm going to go now," he says. He turns to the room. "I'll try some other time. Once I've got a job, and I'm back on my feet."

He turns back to Alvin. "I'll go through proper channels."

"Might be for the best," Alvin says through his crumb-flecked mustache.

"Sorry, man," Darnell says.

"No," Von says. "I don't think so."

Not yet you ain't.

"Hey, man," Darnell catches his arm above the elbow. "We just wanted—"

With his free hand, Von points toward Darnell's. He lifts his eyebrows and says to Alvin, "You seeing this?"

Darnell lets go, lifts his hands in surrender.

"I'm just going to take this." He reaches for his father's Bible, takes it down from its shelf next to the massive TV screen.

I ain't leaving empty-handed. New Von, old Von, doesn't matter: I never leave without taking something. And this shit belongs to me.

The mirror at the back of the shelf reflects his face back to him, and he is genuinely surprised to see how calm he looks, how determined. In control, of himself, and his environment. He almost has to stop and admire himself. His poise. Grace under pressure.

"You don't mind, do you Shelly?"

He turns back toward her.

"This was my father's, after all."

She shrugs. "Go ahead."

"Doesn't look like it's been getting much use," he says, making a show of blowing dust from the top edge, the gilt gleaming dully.

He considers the television console, the gaping hole that he has left there.

Gives them something to remember me by, he thinks. *Like the hole they left in my heart.*

He fights back a smile, as he pulls back on the front door, and pushes through the screen door out into the stifling humidity.

If anything, he has flipped their reality-show-inspired script back on their dumb-asses.

Now he has a gaggle of witnesses, who can attest—under oath, if need be—to the fact that he was completely civil and well-behaved. That he gave these clowns every opportunity to make good. To mend fences. To find some common ground.

To come to a reasonable compromise.

They rigged the game so it would be impossible.

Which they assumed would cause me to flip the fuck out, do something stupid, and get my dumb-ass sent back inside.

They don't know the new me.

The new me is full of surprises.

They're about to find out. All of 'em.

Except Tara, of course. She don't know any better.

She's just a kid.

CHAPTER
THREE

THE BIBLE IS a heavy brick of gilt-edged paper bound in pebbly brown leather rubbed to tan at the corners and along the joints. As soon as he is out of Mandalay Villas he opens the book and flips back to Revelation. Turns every page, but the money is gone. He stops on the sidewalk, pages through the entire New Testament. Spreads the boards apart and lets the pages hang down, gives them a shake. Two blank slips of paper flutter down to the sidewalk. Nothing but bookmarks.

Shit, he thinks. *Bitch stole that from me, too.*

He had put five crispy new one-hundred-dollar bills back there, years ago. As an emergency fund. But fuck it. He can't be sure—there were times back then, with the drugs, where his memory is less than clear. He's just as likely the one who spent it. What was the saying? Robbing from Peter to pay Paul? Shelly would certainly never read a book, much less a big-ass Bible. That was why he used it as a safe spot in the first place.

There are pages at the front titled "Register," where his father's name and date of birth was penned by his father's mother, way back when his father was born. Above his father's name are the names of his three brothers and two sisters, all older than his father, all probably dead by now. He met one of his uncles and the two aunts at his father's funeral, but he was just a boy then. They'd flown in from places like Vermont and Arizona. His father burned some bridges when he got religion and moved down to Florida. "With nothing more than this Bible, the shirt on my back and my belief in the Lord," as he used to say, when he was yelling at Von for being lazy, or whenever Von asked for money for new clothes so he wouldn't get laughed at for being a shitkicker at school.

His name isn't in there. His father had written his mother's name in there, and the date of their marriage, Jan. 23, 1993—seven months before the date of Von's birth—but after that the Register stops. There is no entry for Von, and he never had any siblings. His father always said he had to earn getting his name inscribed in the Good Book, just like in real life.

Then he went and died before Von ever had a chance to prove himself.

He'd taken that lesson to heart, though. Someday he would take a pen and carefully write his own name in there, in full, neater than he ever had at school, and nod and look up to Heaven and know that both his parents were smiling down at him.

He ain't there yet. This whole prison stint was a setback, but he'll overcome it. It was good to reclaim the Bible, because it will remind him. A spur in his side. You got to have goals, isn't that what Mr. Counselor Dude was always saying?

Well, I got myself a goal now.

As he resumes walking, he raps a bar:

Don't care how, by hook or by crook—
gonna write my name in my Pop's Good Book.
Fuckin-A right.

There was another reason to bring the Bible, that he hadn't thought through at the time he'd grabbed it—he just saw it, and knew that he had to have it.

The church isn't far. St. Peter's Evangelical. It's not close —but it's walkable. Pastor Tom will remember him. He'll remember his father, for sure. Best believe every Sunday his pops was there, in the front row, loud and proud, his wife and son meek and quiet by his side.

The sun is low by the time he reaches the church, tucked in among palms and pines. It is much smaller than he remembers, but that's not just him growing up—Hurricane Ian has wrecked shop.

Even the House of the Lord ain't immune.

Most of the outbuildings are gone, including Pastor Tom's house. In its place sits a Sundance trailer, one end on cinder blocks, with an awning that overhangs a dirt patch with a lawn chair, a folding dinner tray, and a square, flat-bottomed charcoal grill. The trailer is dark, but a generator's hum draws Von's attention to the church itself. Portions of the roof are covered in sagging blue tarp, as are sections of the walls. The side door nearest him has been propped open with a brick, and he steps through, into the auditorium.

Two spotlights project their beams up toward the patchy ceiling. A construction scaffold rises toward the blue tarp like a rickety gallows. The chairs are gone, the concrete floor swirled with the remains of dried mud and carpet glue. In the golden light streaming through a gap in the far wall, you could almost imagine it as fancy imported marble, if it weren't for the way it crunched underfoot and lifted puffs of dust with each step.

A tinny voice is speaking, too low for Von to make out the words. A man sits atop the scaffold, wispy white hair and bare shoulders picked out by the spots. As he moves closer, Von can discern the rise and fall of a preaching cadence. The man's head is in his hands. He is shirtless, and his shoulders are knobby, his ribs visible.

"Pastor Tom?" Von's voice hesitates in the cavernous space.

The head disappears; a click silences the preacher's exhortations. A face peers down: long white beard, sunken eyes, cheeks tanned to the color and consistency of old leather.

"I remember you saying the doors to the House of the Lord are always open," Von says, tilting his head back to project his voice toward the ceiling.

"What difference might a door make," Pastor Tom waves a gnarled hand, "when the House of the Lord has no walls?"

Pastor Tom absently scratches his elbow. Angry-looking welts stand out on his bony arms.

"Do you remember me?" Von asks.

"Do you remember the Lord?"

Von hoists the Bible above his head. "I do."

"An empty church is just a roof," the old man says. "An unread Bible is just a book."

"Then I've come to the right place," he says. "I just need a roof over my head, and someone to show me what pages to read."

"When you open your heart, the book opens to the right page."

Dude's lost his marbles, Von thinks. *Ian wiped out more than just the church.*

"Remember my dad? William Martin?"

Pastor Tom leans forward and squints.

"What you said at his funeral really meant a lot."

The scaffold trembles and squeaks as the dirty soles of Pastor Tom's feet swing out over the edge and start working their way down. He wears only dingy sweats cut down to shorts. He is nothing more than skin and bones and beard and bug bites.

And a haunted stare that seems to gaze directly into Von's soul.

"William's boy."

"That's right."

"What did I say before we laid William to rest?"

Von feels called to the front of class to report on a book he hasn't read.

"Something about how the Lord has a plan for all of us," he says. "Even when it seems like he doesn't care."

Pastor Tom scratches at a welt, leaving a streak of dirt or blood.

"Why should he care about us until we begin to care about Him?"

Von can't help but laugh. "If you'd preached like this back in the day," he says, "I might've kept coming to church."

Pastor Tom's bare feet crunch over the filth-strewn floor toward the spotlights.

"I could use a bite to eat, too," Von says, following. "Not gonna lie."

Pastor Tom turns out the first spotlight. "Our belly tells us it's hungry when we do not allow our souls to speak."

He kills the second light, plunging them into near darkness. The sun has set; the golden shafts from earlier have vanished.

"I've been walking all day," Von says, as he follows the old man out the side door. "I done walked that extra mile. And I turned the other cheek."

Pastor Tom's beard twitches—perhaps a hint of a grin.

"If you'd been there, you woulda been proud. Even my pops woulda been proud."

"Seek only your Father's approval," Pastor Tom says as they cross the lawn to his trailer.

Father, with a capital F. I get it, old man. He holds his

tongue though. Exercising self-control. This is the first lesson. Maybe this man can teach him some things.

Pastor Tom steps around the corner of his trailer and returns with a white folding chair, which he unfolds and sets down on the bare ground for Von. He dumps some charcoal into the grill, douses it in lighter fluid, then clicks the trigger on a long lighter and waves it over the briquets until they catch.

Von sits, and he is so tired and sags so deeply into the chair he nearly tips it over. His flailing arms send the Bible flying, to bounce off the side of the trailer and land open in the dirt. Tom peers at him from under bushy eyebrows.

"I'm not drunk or nothing," he says, retrieving the Bible. "Just tired."

"The wicked shall find no rest."

Which kind of pisses Von off, as he brushes and blows dirt from the pages. He's four years sober, after all. Not that he had much choice in the matter, but he made it through. White-knuckled it, especially that first year, but he fucking made it.

"Worse than my dad," he mutters. "Can't say anything right."

Then he freezes, the insult forgotten.

"Yo, check it out!" He holds out the Bible for Pastor Tom to inspect: open to the Book of Job. "You were right—it's just what I need!"

Pastor Tom nods. "Then read," he says. He scrapes his bare feet on the welcome mat, once, twice, thrice, and then steps up and inside.

"Too dark," Von says. He swipes the last of the dirt from the pages, and stretches the silk ribbon into the deep crevice, folds the covers closed, lays his hands over the coarse leather. "Tomorrow."

Pastor Tom steps back out with a pound of hamburger, a plastic sack of buns, and a bottle of ketchup. No cheese, no toppings, but Von isn't about to complain. Isn't about to say anything, at all. Except "Thank you, Lord."

When he says it, he is truly grateful. So grateful he is almost crying.

Maybe that's why Pastor Tom doesn't say anything when Von mumbles his thanks. Maybe that's why he doesn't say anything for the rest of the evening.

Von follows him inside, and stretches himself out on Pastor Tom's cushioned bench. It's not quite long enough, not quite wide enough, but he's been sleeping sound enough on worse for four years now. The air conditioner is right above his head, and when the compressor kicks on it rattles like an airplane prop coughing to life, but for the first time on this very long day his brow finally feels cool, and the noise seems to blast away his ability to think.

He feels something tugging at his feet, and it's Pastor Tom pulling off his Jordans. He almost kicks him, until he realizes the old guy is just on that whole Jesus trip—*just so long as he doesn't try to wash my feet or nothing weird like that*—and he's asleep before Pastor Tom even turns out the light.

CHAPTER
FOUR

VON WAKES with a start into strange surroundings. After four years, wherever he woke up today was bound to feel weird. He slept surprisingly soundly—although, seeing as how he's no longer sleeping in a massive hangar surrounded by a hundred and fifty thieves, junkies, perverts and lowlifes, maybe that shouldn't be such a surprise.

The smell of food draws him into the kitchenette. A small skillet with scrambled eggs and a circular sausage patty sits on the stove.

"Pastor Tom?" he calls out toward the rear room.

No answer. The door is partly open.

He assumes the food has been left for him. Finds a fork, shakes salt and pepper over the skillet, digs in. Turns out the patty is actually twice-cooked hamburger, but that's fine. He finds orange juice in the small fridge—nothing like Florida fresh-squeezed. Better than coffee for jump-starting your day. Though he could use coffee, too. He rummages a bit, comes up empty.

Can't win 'em all.

Outside, the overcast morning makes it seem like it should be cooler, yet it's still disgustingly hot and sticky.

He surveys the church as though it were a worksite he'd been assigned to. It's a wood-framed structure with peaked roofs forming a cross if seen from above. *Needlessly complicated*, he thinks, *making it harder to rebuild*. Around front, in the cracked and weedy parking lot, sits a massive green metal dumpster, partially filled with broken timbers and roofing sections. If he were Pastor Tom, he'd tear it all down to the foundation, start over with concrete and rebar and cinder blocks. Make it hurricane-proof.

Once in a hundred years. That's what they said about Ian.

The glass front doors and windows have been replaced with plywood panels. He slips into the darkness through the side door.

Banging echoes through the empty auditorium. Pastor Tom has returned to his perch atop the scaffolding. He's stretching up toward Heaven, hammer in his fist, nailing framing into place.

"You doing all this yourself?" Von asks during a break in the hammering.

Pastor Tom peers down through the dim.

"Seems like a big job for one person," Von adds.

"He who walks with the Lord never walks alone."

"Maybe I can help out this afternoon," Von says. "But there's somebody I have to see, about a job. Remember how the Bible fell open to the Book of Job last night? Tell me that ain't my pops telling me I need to get one."

"Plenty of work here."

"Yeah, I can see that. But I need to get paid, you know?"

"He who walks with the Lord lays up his treasure in Heaven," the old man says, "for the end is nigh."

"I hear you, Pastor Tom." Von's neck is already stiffening

from tilting his head back. "But I need an actual job if I want to see my daughter. The courts want to see an address and a paystub. Gotta go through proper channels."

"The Lord provideth."

"I sure hope so."

"And the Lord taketh away."

Yeah, whatever.

Von turns to go, but then a question occurs to him, and he turns back around.

"Hey, Pastor Tom. Where can I find that verse about an eye for an eye?"

That's in the Bible, right? While eating his eggs, he'd leafed through the book, and it occurred to him that it would be pretty bad-ass if he had a line to quote, the way Samuel L. Jackson does in that movie, the wild one with John Travolta and Bruce Willis, the one where homeboy gets his head blown off in the back seat of a car by accident. Now that was some funny shit.

"The whole world is already blind," the old man says, unhelpfully.

"Or what about that one about walking a mile in my shoes?"

"If someone forces you to go one mile, go with him two miles. Matthew 5:41."

"You sure? Wasn't there one about walking in my shoes though? That's what these assholes should do—walk a mile in these Jordans. See how they like it."

Pastor Tom sits on the scaffolding ledge, letting his filthy feet dangle, resting his forearms on one of the bars, his bearded chin on his forearms.

"Do you know the saying about revenge?" he asks.

"It's best served cold, right?" Von brightens. "Is that one in there? That would be perfect."

Maybe not to say to people, but for himself. A motto. A

mantra. Positive self-talk, like Mr. Counselor Dude was always on about.

Pastor Tom winces and shakes his beard. "Before setting out on a journey of revenge, be sure to dig two graves."

Von chuckles, shakes his head.

"Pastor Tom, if this guy was setting out for revenge, best believe you'd have to dig more than two graves. A *lot* more. But don't worry—I ain't about revenge. I'm all about respect now. That's *my* journey. The Good Book is my guide, and my pops is watching down over me. He led me to you, Pastor Tom, I know he did. Him and the good Lord."

He waves over his shoulder to Pastor Tom, telling him he'll try to make it back by the afternoon to give him a hand. He feels bad for the old coot. But not so bad that he's just going to take over the old man's project for him and work for three hots and a cot—but no green.

Been doing quite enough of that these past four years, thank you very much. Not one day more. No sir.

Back in the trailer, in a closet he finds an old black suit jacket, matching slacks, and a white button-down Oxford all sharing the same hanger, with a skinny black tie looped under the shirt collar. From the coating of dust on the jacket's shoulders, it would seem that Pastor Tom hasn't worn this getup in quite some time.

He tries it on. The shirt is snug in the chest, the jacket pinches at the shoulders. The sleeves and pant legs fall a little short. But when he puts the tie on, and looks in the mirror—

Damn if you ain't the spitting image of John Travolta in that movie. Just without the pony tail. Fuckin-A. Too cool for school, bro.

In the back of the closet he finds black leather loafers. These aren't just tight—these are *small*.

They're leather, he tells himself. *They should stretch.*

He's borrowing this stuff for the day. *Ain't like Pastor*

Tom's gonna be wearing it to work on his roof. He'll take the suit to the dry cleaners when he's done.

I'll leave my Jordans as collateral. My Jordans and the Bible. So the old man knows I'm good for it.

As he strides across the parking lot, Von has every intention of returning to help Pastor Tom rebuild his roof.

He catches a bus that gets him most of the way across town. While riding he removes the jacket, folds it onto the seat beside him, kicks off Pastor Tom's shoes. By the time he arrives at the home office of RTG Construction, he's not sweating too badly. He takes a moment in the lobby bathroom to splash water on his face, pat himself dry with paper towels. Drinks three cups of water from the cooler. Then presents himself to the desk.

He doesn't recognize the girl behind it, but she sure is a babe, silver cross bouncing around on the trampoline between her breasts formed by her clinging sleeveless turtleneck. Raul always had an eye for talent.

"Is Raul in?" Casual.

"Do you have an appointment?"

"Nah, don't need one." He winks. "I'm an old friend. We go way back."

"He's pretty booked up today. What's your name?"

"Von," he says. "Von Martin."

"Von? How do you—"

"He'll know," he says. "I helped build this place."

She lifts the phone hesitantly, presses a button. "Hey, it's Gina. I've got a guy here, says he's an old friend." She holds her hand over the receiver, mouths to Von, "He might be out at a job site."

"What's the good word?" Von asks, after he's been

standing there a while. Gina holds up her finger, nods along to the receiver, jostling that little silver crucifix.

"Thanks, hun," she says, voice suddenly nasal. "That's what I thought—he's out at a job site."

"Any idea when he'll be back?"

"This afternoon? Sometime? She didn't know for sure."

"Maybe I should talk to her—"

"She's in a meeting—you're welcome to wait here, for as long as you'd like."

"I'll wait a bit. But I've got a shit-ton to do today."

"I understand," Gina says. She's done with him.

The lobby is as frigid as Gina is smoking hot, so Von figures he'll take a load off, cool down a bit. Unfortunately, once he sits he can only see the crown of Gina's head. He gets up, drinks some more water. Spends time in the men's room, cleaning and drying himself. On the back of the toilet is a spray bottle of eau de cologne—he hits himself with a blast under each arm, on his chest. The poor man's shower. Back in the lobby he flips through magazines—all touting the benefits of living in sunny Florida: blue skies, white beaches, green and red cocktails, tan skin and bright teeth.

Come see old Von, he thinks, as he turns the pages. *I'll give you a pro for every con.* The thought makes him chuckle.

After an hour, it's clear he's getting nowhere. The heat is rising within him again, defeating the purpose of sitting in AC. He stands, and strides toward Gina.

"I've got to scoot to my next appointment," he says, wishing he had a Rolex he could glance down at.

"Would you like to leave a phone number? I could have him call you—"

"Nah, that's okay. I'll catch him later. Just let the big guy know I stopped by."

"Will do, Mr... Martin?"

"Just Von," he says. "He'll know. Best believe."

With a wink, he's out the door. An air-conditioned halo accompanies him for a few steps before the sticky humidity presses in, shrinks it, collapses it around him until it evaporates, leaving him exposed. By the time he reaches the main road, he's sweating again.

CHAPTER FIVE

IT'S late afternoon when Von reaches the entrance to Bay Mar Estates, the name in brass lettering behind a sheet of endlessly falling water. He sits on a low rise in the manicured lawn at the fringe of the flowerbeds, hidden by palmettos from the gatehouse but with a clear view of vehicles turning into the development. Beemers, Porsches, Mercedes—no surprise. The surprising thing is they're all SUVs. Even a Lambo SUV. *Who buys a Lambo SUV?* he wonders. *Someone with more money than sense.*

As he waits, he worries this might be in vain. The service vehicles stop at the gatehouse, but residents breeze by on an outer lane, slowing only for an arm triggered by a transponder. The driver-side window often rolls down for a wave to the schlub on duty, but the passenger side stays up, darkly tinted against the Florida sun.

Boy could he use some water. Even in the shade, the heat is stifling. His shirt plastered to his back.

There are no benches—the last thing they want is to encourage lowlifes like him to sit out front, gawking. He's picked a spot out the gatehouse's line of sight, but he knows it's only a matter of time before some jackass in a blue Bay Mar polo comes out to tell him he's on private property.

There. A massive black SUV—an Escalade or Expedition—with "RTG Construction" lettered on the side, slowing into the right turn. He can't see through the tinted passenger window, but he's got to shoot his shot.

"Raul," he says, rising. "Raul!" Legs stiff, he hobbles quickly toward the curb, waves his arms. "Hey, yo! Raul!"

The car is still moving fast, slowing only for the curve.

"Raul!"

He's close enough to smack the rear passenger door—didn't time it quite right, his damn legs were too stiff.

Brake lights. *Thank God.*

The passenger window lowers silently. Von steps to it.

Raul. His former boss. The thick dark hair that he was always so proud of shows delicate touches of gray at the temples. His five o'clock shadow stands out darkly on his tanned skin.

"Hey," Von says, catching his breath. "Raul."

Dark eyes glare fiercely at him from beneath bushy eyebrows; thick lips purse into a scowl.

"It's me. Von."

"So I see. When'd you get out?"

"Just yesterday."

"No shit? Well, welcome back. Back in the real world, right?"

"Back in the suck," Von nods. "I was hoping we could talk."

A car horn beeps from behind.

"You got us holding up traffic," Raul says.

Von raises his hand and says "Just a minute" to the Porsche convertible stopped behind them.

"I went by the office," Von says. "To go through proper channels. But they said you were out."

"I'm often out."

"So I figured I'd find you here."

"You found me."

The driver—a heavyset younger man, with dark eyes and hair but pale skin, looks like he might've played lineman for Florida International—lowers his window and waves toward the gatehouse. Letting them know they don't need to send the cavalry.

"Can we talk?" Von asks. "Just for a moment."

"Hop in." Raul hooks his thumb toward the seat behind him, and the window glides up.

Von waves thanks at the car behind—the occupants, retired geezers in sun visors, are studiously ignoring him now. *Probably terrified I'll ask them for money.*

But I ain't asking for a handout. I'm asking for a fucking job. Big difference.

The door unlocks with a *kerchunk*, and Von climbs in. Before he can close the door properly, he's pressed back into the leather seat as the car zooms forward. The driver waves again at the gatehouse while they wait for the striped arm to lift, and then they're through, driving down palm-lined avenues flanked by fairways and sand traps.

He'd been to Raul's Bay Mar mansion before—several times—though always as an employee working on the renovations. That was back when he first started on Raul's crew.

But Raul tells the driver to take them to the clubhouse. They're deposited at the front door, and the maître d' seems overjoyed to see Mr. Gimenez. He leads them past a horseshoe-shaped bar bustling with rich geezers, through a dining room, into a dim lounge with circular tables and low leather chairs. An actual fire burns in the fireplace, countering the cranked AC.

"Everybody looks like Coach leather and smells like Gold Bond," Von cracks, as the maître d' pulls back Raul's chair.

"Not really my crowd," Raul says, once they're seated. "But the food is fantastic."

Raul orders an old-fashioned, made with rye; Von is tempted to order the same—double—but asks for tonic water.

"Not drinking anymore," he says.

"Good for you."

"Turns out the joint was good for me, in a lot of ways," Von continues. "Really gave me time to think, you know? Made me realize it's time to get my head on straight, and fly right."

Raul lifts his eyebrows. "Glad to hear it, Von."

A cute girl sets their drinks down while another brings menus, but Raul waves them away.

He claps Von's shoulder. "Bring this man your best and biggest porterhouse—medium, but we want to see a little pink, right?—with those garlic mashed potatoes and creamed spinach. We'll start with the shrimp cocktail, and a dozen oysters—whatever's freshest. But briny, right? I'll have the steak salad, hold the croutons and onions, dressing on the side. And a baked sweet potato with butter and maple syrup. I know you got the real stuff back there. Got all that?"

"Creamed spinach?" Von asks after she's gone.

"Trust me now, thank me later," Raul says.

I like that line, Von thinks. *Should remember that.*

Raul lifts his squat cut-crystal rocks glass with its amber liquid and massive ice cube glowing in the firelight, taps it against Von's taller, slimmer glass, full of fizzy nothing.

"To flying straight," Raul says.

"Amen, brother."

The shrimp arrive. Von's mouth floods with saliva. He reaches for one, dunks it deep in cocktail sauce.

Von closes his eyes, savors the chilled sweetness and peppery heat.

"This is like the perfect antidote to my day," he says. "Tromping all over creation."

Raul plucks an oyster from an elevated, ice-filled tray, dresses it with lemon and mignonette, knocks it back. For a few minutes, they slurp and chew in silence.

"So you're out now, eh?" Raul says. "Freedom is a wonderful thing."

"Yep."

"That was my big takeaway from upstate," Raul says. "Nothing so valuable as your freedom. Doesn't matter how much you lost, how much it set you back—you're out now, and that's worth its weight in gold bars."

"I'm never going back," Von says.

"No way," Raul says. "There is nothing you could offer me that might tempt me to risk it. Nothing anyone could say that would get me off the straight and narrow." He lifts his nearly empty glass, waves it over the last few shrimp and oysters. "And give this up? No way."

"You know, I never cared much for oysters," Von says.

"No?" Raul interrupts. "Sure are packing them away." Busting his balls—but with a gentle laugh.

"I just realized why they taste so good to me now," Von says. "They taste like freedom."

Raul slurps back the last one, closes his eyes.

"You are so right," he says. He waves his empty glass at the waitress. She asks Von if he wants another tonic, and he's this close to changing his order to match Raul's. But he holds off. Another tonic water. Please.

Be consistent. Self-control. Job first. Then celebrate.

It's just that every fiber in his being wants to celebrate being out, and wants to celebrate it *now*. The last four years was a hell of a job, after all. He made it through, dignity intact. With a newfound self-respect.

Respect yourself first and foremost, Mr. Counselor Dude always said. *Respect from others will follow.*

"Remind me," Raul says. "You got a kid, right?"

Von nods. "Tara. Saw her yesterday."

"That's right." Raul repeats her name. "How is she?"

"She's beautiful. She's six now. Can't believe I'm even saying that."

"That's great. So you know how it is. Last thing you want to do is fuck up now, right? Every day I'm not in that place, I don't care how shitty it is, how much shit some client makes me eat, I thank the good Lord I'm here and not back in that hellhole."

"Jesus," Von says. "Between you and Pastor Tom, I'm getting a full week of Sunday sermons in two days."

"Pastor Tom?"

"Some guy I'm staying with. Friend of my dad's." One of the waitresses whisks away his oyster shells. "He's read the Bible so much it's gone to his head."

"Well, listen to that guy, then," Raul says. "Not me."

The other waitress slides an enormous steak in front of him. The buttery-salty smell of rendered fat causes a whole other set of salivary glands, back by his throat, to well up in anticipation.

Von rubs his hands together, reaches for his fork and knife.

Raul's phone rattles and crawls sideways on the table.

"Excuse me," he says, pushing back. "I gotta take this. You good?"

"Sure."

"Anything else you want, just let Marcella know."

Marcella smiles and waves from across the room.

The steak is done to perfection. The potatoes go down like clouds of whipped garlic butter. He pokes at the creamed spinach—not a fan of either ingredient, and together they threaten to turn his stomach. He pushes the dish away, focuses on the steak.

There are only a couple of other parties in the lounge, plus a younger couple with kids on the leather bench between them.

Imagine growing up with this as your everyday, Von thinks. Then: *No—don't imagine that. That's how you start down the negativity spiral.*

Be content. Be grateful. Be in the moment, as Mr. Counselor Dude would say.

By the time Raul returns, Von has made a point of chewing each bite thoroughly, leaving some on his plate. Doesn't want to seem like a feral human who hasn't seen a decent meal in four years. Raul apologizes as he sits, scoops a glop of the spinach mess onto his plate, dunks steak bits forked from his salad into it.

"It might seem tough at first, staying straight," Raul says, chewing. "But after a while you get used to it. Hell, you get to a certain point in business where you're making more money than you ever could being crooked."

He frowns, glances at Von.

"Don't get me wrong—it's a lot of work. I bust my ass. I'm just saying I'd never be tempted to do anything shady again."

Von leans back and laughs. "Don't worry, boss. I ain't the devil, come to tempt you."

"No, I know. It's all about keeping your head down and your nose clean."

"That's my motto these days. A steady job would make that a hundred times easier."

Raul nods, chews. Swallows.

"Yeah, I hear you," he says. He takes a long last sip of his old-fashioned. That big square cube rattles the cut crystal. "Drop your resume off at the office. I'm sure we can—"

"My resume? You serious?"

"Look, Von, I can't just—"

"After the way I held down the fort when you were upstate?"

Those bushy eyebrows hunch lower.

"After you did what now?"

"Who kept your Bonita and Pelican Bay crews in line when you were away?"

"Uh, Michael. Bonnie."

"Yeah, but who did they rely on to talk Spanish to the workers and keep their lazy asses in line? Maybe they never said nothing because they wanted to take all the credit, but that was me."

Marcella comes by asking how everything is. "Great," Raul says. "Just the check, when you get a chance."

She skips away. *I guess no dessert*, Von thinks.

"Look, everything has to be above board now," Raul says. "No more under the table shit."

He was convicted on fraud and tax evasion, maybe eight years ago. *Fifteen months—with time served—in minimum security? What does he know about doing time?*

"I've got demo projects out the wazoo, still cleaning up after Ian up in Fort Myers Beach and Sanibel. I'm sure we'll find something."

"Demo?"

"You'll have to work like a Mexican, but coming out of the joint, that's just what a man needs, right? An honest day's work for an honest day's pay. That's how you keep your nose clean."

"I'm more of a construction guy than demo."

"You gotta work your way up. Like anywhere else. You prove yourself, you advance."

So now I gotta prove myself, to you? We all gotta bow down to Mr. Bigshot Raul Tomás Gimenez, who's now some country club Republican pull-yourself-up-by-your-bootstraps blowhard.

Raul hands Marcella a black credit card, watches her ass swish away, then turns back to Von. From his gunmetal money clip he peels first one, then two, then—after a hitch—a third bill and slides them across.

Hundreds. They feel crisp and new.

"To get you over the hump," Raul says.

Raul stands. Von joins him. Raul has a good couple inches on him, maybe fifty pounds.

"You've been living well." Von folds the bills, tucks them into his pocket. "Much appreciated."

Raul is thumbing his phone as he leads the way out. The tables are largely empty, staff resetting them for breakfast. The picture windows are black.

The maître d' holds the door as they step into the humid night.

"You headed to this Pastor's place? Ern will take you anywhere you want to go."

"That's cool. No need to trouble. I'll walk."

"Nah," Raul says, as Ern glides the enormous SUV to the curb. Raul opens the rear door for Von. "We probably shouldn't do that. Wouldn't want you getting picked up by security—it's pretty tight around here. They don't like people they don't know walking around after dark."

Von hauls himself up and in, very aware of his full belly.

Raul opens the passenger door, says to the driver, take our friend wherever he wants to go.

Ern looks up into the rear view. "Where to, pal?"

"Tarzan's."

Raul leans into the doorway to catch Von's eye, lifts his eyebrows. "Thought you weren't drinking these days?"

"Just to say hi to Howie. It's been a minute."

"Wasn't one of the dancers there into you, too?" Raul asks. "What was her name?"

"Oh yeah." That's right. He'd totally forgotten. "What *was* her name?"

He'd been so focused on Shelly and what a rotten bitch she'd turned out to be that he'd forgotten all about...

"I mean, I'm sure it wasn't her real name," Raul says.

"Jasmine," Von says. *That was it.*

"Jasmine. Right. Maybe she's still dancing there."

"Could be."

"Well, good luck with Jasmine, or whoever else is there. I know how it is, first days out. Just remember: head down, nose clean."

"You got it, boss."

"I'm going back inside, gonna hit on Marcella again. She'll come around, one of these days."

Raul closes the door, waves. Heads back in.

Ern waits while an older couple crosses in front, then puts the boat into gear and guides them slowly through the parking lot.

CHAPTER
SIX

"LET ME OFF HERE," Von says, before they've gone very far. He wants out.

"Mr. G said you're going to Tarzan's," Li'l Ern says.

"I changed my mind."

"Mr. G didn't change his mind."

"Bro," Von says. "Man to man. I just got out of the joint. Four fucking years since the last time I broke me off a piece. I know a little cutie up here in Pelican Bay who is DTF. Just drop me off here."

Li'l Ern takes some persuading, but Von wears him down. He hits the brakes and gives Von just enough time to step down before tearing off, the acceleration slamming the door closed. Von jumps back to keep the rear wheel from running over his foot.

"Dickhead," he says—but he's smiling. He got his way. He sets off walking.

And now guess who's coming back, Raul.

You might've gotten rich since I been gone, but you also went and got soft. It's written all over you, with your jewelry, your watch, your haircut, your manicure. Your dumb-ass "chauffeur."

My resume. Ain't that a bitch.

You know who has to go through proper channels? A poor motherfucker just outta the joint like me, that's who. I ain't got a choice, 'cause I ain't got a lawyer. Ain't got a company. And I certainly ain't got a resume. Even if I did, all it's ever going to say is "don't hire this convict."

Come on, bro. Be real.

There was a time when a guy would get out of the joint, and his boss would say, hey, welcome home. Glad you're back. I appreciate the sacrifices you've made. You kept your head down and your mouth shut. Of course I got work for a man with your talents.

You of all people, Raul! You did time yourself!

Not real time—not like I put in—but you know what it's like!

And you're going to tell me come back on Monday, and bring my resume? My life on a flimsy piece of paper? What the fuck, bro? We were brothers! We were in the trenches together! We were a crew!

But there are people who will take advantage of you, when they know you're from the streets. When they know you're a stand-up guy, when they know you won't rat them out, no matter what kind of trumped-up charges the man throws at you. They know you're going to do your bid and keep your mouth shut. Meanwhile they're out here, free as a bird, eating their oysters, plowing their secretaries, having a laugh at your expense.

The big guy eats the pie, and us little guys get the crumbs.

Von turns from Vanderbilt into the residential side streets, continues heading south.

But you've underestimated me, Raul. Big time. Von Martin ain't the kind of guy who's just gonna bend over and take it. Best believe. I didn't give it up in the joint—I sure as hell ain't about to bend over like a bitch out here.

There was a time when I looked up to you, like a father figure. That's why I never said A WORD about how you knew what I was doing, THE WHOLE GODDAMN TIME, even if that would've gotten me a reduced sentence. Because Von ain't a little bitch like that. I knew what I had to do, and I did it. Yet somehow you can't bring yourself to return the fucking favor.

My resume.

He reaches the end of the development. Finds a house that is dark, with no cars in the driveway. He swiftly crosses the gravel yard and plunges into the sparse underbrush behind the house.

Three hundred bucks. You think that's enough to buy me? How many times did I break you off a Benjamin or two, as your cut, when you did absolutely nothing except come whining to me about how I gotta knock this shit off? Best believe, I see your game now: it was all an act, wasn't it? To get me to cough up some bills, which you were more than happy to take.

A man's actions, Raul, not his words.

That's what I'm judging you by: your actions.

He comes to a wall, eight feet tall, fronted by shrubs and overgrown with firebush. He forces his way between the wall and the shrubs, finds a spot for his foot in the narrow crook of two branches, then gripping handfuls of firebush, he boosts himself up to the top of the wall. Drops down on the other side.

Back in Bay Mar Estates.

How many times did I spring for bottle service at Tarzan's, for you and the whole crew? You were more than happy to drink my tequila then, weren't you, Raul? More than happy to have Jasmine give you a lap dance then, weren't you?

You remember. Four years may be a long-ass time in a lot of other ways, but it ain't so long that you just go and forget.

Best believe I ain't forgotten.
Your boy Von don't forget a single goddamn thing.

Raul's mansion looms up out of the shadows at the end of a spur of land that projects into the inlet. It's a prime piece of property. He's smart when it comes to evaluating real estate. It's when it comes to evaluating people, that's where he's suspect.

Von knows Raul hates dogs—one less thing to worry about.

There's the Escalade, sitting in the broad circular driveway. Along with an Alfa Romeo coupe, black, or maybe dark green, hard to tell in the orange lights. Buildings along the waterfront can't have white lights, because it disorients baby turtles. Draws them like moths to the flame, apparently.

Which is kind of how he feels, with his heart in his mouth, moving around the perimeter of the property, keeping to the shadows along the wall, hiding behind bushes. Knowing he shouldn't be here. But also knowing that Raul is in there, somewhere, sleeping like a baby, without a care in the world—because he assumes that Von is soft, like he is.

Because he now plays by the rules, he assumes that I'm going to play by those same rules.

But like Mr. Counselor Dude liked to say, we all grow up learning different rules.

Still Von waits. It's not late enough, not yet. He might be banging that Marcella chick. Hell, he might be banging Li'l Ern. Who knows.

He's figured his route in. There are three floors, but really only two, as the ground floor is purely for vehicles and guest rooms. This is the sacrificial floor that the sea will claim when the next hurricane whips the water into a frenzy and swamps the coast. The ground floor hides the solid concrete and rebar columns that support the real house. He spots a tree he can climb, a branch of which will deposit him onto a balcony. From there, he's certain he'll find an unlocked door or window. Hell, there's a thirty percent chance this chump hasn't even locked his front door. Von knows how it is in these gated communities. That's how he wrecked shop, for so long.

I always suspected Darnell was the one who ratted me out. Because of Shelly.

But maybe I should've been suspicious of someone even closer. Someone who really knew what I was up to.

Someone who had even more to lose.

Raul didn't want to lose his precious company, and all his precious money. Darnell only wanted to gain Shelly.

Which—let's be real—ain't such a prize.

The doors from the balcony are locked, but he finds a window that slides open easily, quietly, giving into a bathroom. A little butterfly nightlight glowing blue reveals two sinks, a walk-in shower, no clutter—a guest bathroom, off the main hallway. He tries to remember the layout from the few times he was here laying floorboards and hanging drywall, before it was furnished.

He cracks open the door. The house is dark, and hushed. A low hum emerges from a dehumidifier set into the wall.

This isn't about a big score. He wants to boost something valuable, of course—he's gonna get paid for his trouble. But it doesn't have to be a huge payday. Nothing that's going to be any trouble to unload.

Better something small—something personal, though. A thing to let him know, subconsciously, that something is missing.

Just like something is missing for me. Something you took from me, Raul.

He knows exactly where he's going to find it. Raul had

what he liked to call a trophy room. Den, man cave, library, bar—he called it his trophy room.

There was a bottle of brandy that Von remembers him bragging about. Not to his employees, of course—he always tried to hide his wealth from his employees. But Von overheard him talking about it on the phone, to some client he was trying to impress. A bottle of brandy that supposedly came from Napoleon's own bar, from that island where they held him prisoner.

Why this is so great, Von never understood. Like buying a bottle of champagne from the Spurs locker room after losing to the Heat. Sure, they won some—but not that year. Not when it counted.

Now, this would be tricky to unload. He's sure that there are papers that go with it, to establish provenance. Who's going to want to buy that from him? Howie wouldn't touch it.

But he's not going to sell it.

He's going to drink it.

Even if it does taste like shit—even if it's skunked—he'll still enjoy every last sip. Knowing he's just pissing away thousands of Raul's ill-gotten dollars.

Too perfect.

The staircase stands at the front of the house, dividing the living room and the dining room. He makes his way through the kitchen, softly lit by touchscreens on both the range and the refrigerator that flicker to life as he passes nearby. He pauses at the knife block, considers grabbing a weapon—just in case—but that's not his style. He's not a violent man. He knows how to hurt Raul in ways that leave no physical trace.

The staircase is a beautiful wooden spiral structure that seems to float its way up through the heart of the home. He reaches the first step, stares up, into complete darkness. He's going to have to wait for his eyes to adjust. He steadies himself, hand on the railing. His breathing is slow. The house is as silent as a morgue. The sort of silence he never experienced in the joint. Never a truly quiet moment.

He doesn't see it, or even hear it—he just senses movement. Above, on the steps. He turns to retrace his steps through the kitchen, when all the lights in the house blast on.

The effect is like a flash-bang grenade: the light flooding into his overly dilated pupils stuns him. The harsh glare keeps him from seeing where he's going.

Besides, he knows he's cooked. Running is only going to make it worse.

He hears the footfalls on the staircase behind him. A cold hard finger presses into the place where his skull meets his spine. He raises his hands to shoulder height.

"On your knees, shithead." *Li'l Ern*, he thinks.

Von complies. There is no carpet here, no rug, to shield his knees from the hardwood floor.

"Vonny boy." Raul's voice draws his attention to the living room. He rises from a deep leather chair over by the fireplace, which is surrounded by gray interlocking stones that stretch to the vaulted ceiling. Von remembers now that the living room was open through the third floor; the master suite looks down from the top of the staircase.

"Nice place," Von says. "Your interior designer has excellent taste."

"Shut up," Li'l Ern says.

Raul crosses the living room, slowly. Reluctantly. He is wearing a white bathrobe. His eyes are bleary and bloodshot. As he approaches, he runs his left hand through his disheveled hair. His right hand remains in the robe's pocket, wrapped around a bulge.

"Your Brazilian Tigerwood." Von lowers his right hand to the floor. "It's holding up real nice." Reminding Raul that he's the one who laid these floorboards down.

"Hands up, thief." Li'l Ern buries the barrel so far into the nape of his neck that he has to use both hands to catch himself as he pitches forward. A hand grabs his shirt collar, hauls him back up.

"Vonny boy, Vonny boy," Raul says. "You done fucked up, Vonny boy."

He is cooked. He knows it. *Get on with it.*

"This is a stand-your-ground state," Raul continues. "I have every right to put a bullet in your brain."

But he knows that they aren't about to do anything to make a mess on his bare hardwood. They're going to want to move him first.

In the meantime, we can talk. Man to man.

"I need a place to stay, Raul," Von says.

Raul snorts. "Oh, is that what you're looking for? Creeping through my house at four in the morning? You're looking for a bed? I don't think so."

"Should I call the cops?" another, deeper voice asks, from behind Raul.

Three of them. Shit.

Raul's eyes lift from Von to someplace behind his right shoulder. Then back to Von.

"That's a very good question, isn't it, Vonny boy? You want a bullet between your beady little eyes? Or you want to go back to the big house?"

"C'mon—don't do me like that. We used to be brothers, man."

"Brothers?"

He nods at Li'l Ern, and the gun barrel pushes him forward again, until his forehead is against the hardwood. And he keeps pushing. Until his nose and his cheek are pressed into the floorboards that he hammered into place. The barrel shifts to his cheek.

"You have the gall to pull that guilt shit on me about

brothers?"

"I know," Von mumbles, working his jaw against the floor. "I know—I'm a shithead"

Raul leans down over him.

"You are so fucking predictable," he hisses. "You think I didn't know what seeing you again meant?"

"You sure called it, boss," Li'l Ern says.

"I hoped you would prove me wrong," Raul continues. "But I'll tell you what, Vonny boy. I may not always be right. But with a little lowlife pinhead twerp like you, assume the worst, and you'll never be wrong."

Twerp? Somehow, this is the most insulting thing he's ever been called.

"This will be real prison, too, and for a much longer time. You get your shit pushed in upstate?"

Von shakes his head, grunts.

"Well, where you'll be going this time, they're gonna love your sweet ass."

"Have the decency—" he tries to say. The pressure relents a touch, so he can speak. "Have the decency to kill me before you do me like that."

"Where's my money?" Raul has straightened.

"Wha?"

"The three hundred dollars I gave you out of the generosity of my heart."

Von slides his right hand back toward his hip pocket. A black work boot steps on his wrist, while a hand pats his ass cheek, then reaches into the pocket. Extracts his money.

"Three hundred and twenty-two," the deeper voice says.

"I'm taking back the three hundred," Raul says. "But I'm not taking a penny more. You understand Von? I'm not taking anything from you that I didn't give you in good faith. So we are square. You got that?"

Von nods, as best he can. "Mmff," he mumbles.

"And if I ever set eyes on you again," he says, "I will squash you like the cockroach you are."

Again, Von moves his head against the floor.

Raul reaches down, places his hand over the gun barrel, lifts it from his cheek. He squats down, forcing Von to take in his tighty-whities beneath his robe.

"Are we square, Von?"

Von nods.

"I want to hear you say it."

"We're square, Raul."

He waits for a punch, or spit, or some last parting shot. Instead Raul stands, and walks into the kitchen. Von hears what sounds like a rocks glass clunk down on the marble countertop. Which he also installed.

"Get that piece of shit out of my sight."

"You got it, boss," Li'l Ern says.

Hands grab him roughly under the shoulders, haul him to his feet. Turns out Li'l Ern was an appropriate nickname, as the second thug is even taller, broader, and fatter. *You must be Big Ern*, Von thinks. They sandwich him, take him out the front doors, down the sweeping stone steps to the waiting Escalade. They throw him in the back, tell him to lie on the floor between the seats, as they don't want him shitting up the upholstery. Li'l Ern gets behind the wheel, and Big Ern sits in the back, resting his boots on Von's shoulders and the small of his back.

At least the floor liners are clean. He can smell the plastic —maybe they're even new.

They drive in silence. Von even finds himself dozing off, as the adrenaline leaves his body, what with the gentle rocking of the vehicle and the roaring hum of the highway racing beneath him. They pull to a stop, and the door opens, the pressure lifts from his back. Hands drag him from the vehicle, throw him down on the side of the road, sending him rolling into a culvert. Like trash.

"Consider yourself lucky," Big Ern intones, from above.

The two thugs climb back into the SUV. Maneuvering the vehicle on this narrow road requires several turns and reverses. When they are finally pointed back in the direction they came from, the brake lights flash, and the driver side window lowers.

"Pray we don't see you again," Li'l Ern says. Then, with a shower of gravel and a cloud of dirt, the big SUV roars away.

Von climbs out of the culvert, stands in the middle of a road of packed earth, watches the taillights slowly shrink away into the night. Behind him, a touch of brightness at the horizon. Dawn is breaking over the Everglades, and with it a cacophony of bird calls. He has himself a piss, and begins the long walk back to civilization.

You're right, Raul, he thinks. *I am a cockroach.*

But you know what a cockroach does? He survives.

By the time he reaches the highway, the sky has brightened and he can see the road in front of him, but the sun remains hidden by the low-hanging clouds. Which just means the morning humidity won't burn off. He's sweating.

These preacher shoes are killing me. He takes them off. With one in each hand, he keeps on walking.

You know who's going to outlast the nuclear apocalypse?

Me, that's who. Me and all the other cockroaches. Because we don't give a shit. We're survivors. That's who we are. It's in our DNA. We're just built different.

CHAPTER
SEVEN

THE SUN IS SETTING by the time Von arrives at Tarzan's. That's after having hitched a ride in the back of a Mexican's pickup, and then borrowed a balloon-tire beach bike. Not one of those powered bikes he's been seeing everywhere, though—this one he actually has to pedal. He leaves it at the back of Tarzan's parking lot, behind a dumpster. Maybe it'll still be there later. But probably not.

They're just opening up. Howie's not even in yet, so Von takes a seat at the end of the bar, asks for water with ice and a lime, knocks it back. He's painfully aware, as he scans the menu, that twenty-two dollars barely even gets you a burger anymore.

One good thing about being in the joint: you ain't gotta deal with bullshit like inflation.

Howie sweeps in through the front door, two hundred eighty pounds in a floral shirt and linen shorts. Head down, he's about to breeze past until Von snags his shirt and calls out his name.

He stops, frowns, then brightens. "Hey, Von!" He claps him on the shoulder. "When'd you get out?"

"Two days ago."

"You been partying ever since or what?"

"Something like that."

"You come in last night? I didn't see you—but it was crazy here."

Von shakes his head. "Business is good, then?"

"Eh." Howie shrugs. "If I thought I could sell this place I would. Too many headaches."

"I hear ya, bro," Von says. Though he's pretty sure he'd trade Howie's headaches for his own any day of the week. "Hey man—I got a favor to ask you."

"Yeah, of course."

Back in high school, Howie had been a couple years behind Von. One day Von was minding his own business, smoking a cigarette under the bleachers, absently watching a kid from his class picking on Howie. He was a big kid, even as a freshman, but this older guy kept pushing him around. Von didn't know which infuriated him more—the asshat doing the bullying, or Howie for putting up with it. Von walked over, and when the punk asked him what he was looking at, he said, "A dead man, you don't leave this kid alone." The other guy thought about, then shrugged and walked away.

"A big kid like you shouldn't be letting yourself get pushed around," Von had told him.

For the rest of the year, he made Howie his project: whipping him into shape, making a man out of this overgrown spineless pudge-ball. It was good for both of them—actually gave Von a reason to keep attending.

Because he was a nice guy—even if to a fault—Howie did have a lot of friends. And so Von, as the older guy, would get beer for their parties, and sell them bags of shake and coke cut with baking powder and scalped concert tickets. Further motivation. At these parties he learned that some of their parents were very into high-end stereo equipment, and he ran a very profitable sideline in speculating on said gear. Not to mention a less profitable but just as entertaining sideline in fucking their girlfriends because he was a senior and a bad boy and made sure he always had a baggie of actual uncut coke on him. By the end of the year even these dweebs were starting to put two and two together and he was running out of excuses, but he was about to graduate anyway, and knew he wasn't going to see any of them ever again.Through it all, Howie stuck up for him, insisted he was a stand-up guy.

He never did see any of those snooty assholes again—except for Howie. The one person in his life who actually treated him like a friend. Who actually deserved to be called that.

"You eat yet?" Howie asks. Before Von can answer, Howie calls the bartender over. "Bring this man a burger and a beer. You want anything on that? Cheese? Bacon?"

Von can barely nod. So goddamn hungry, the thought of a burger and a beer nearly makes him cry.

"On the house," Howie tells the bartender. "This is Von. Whatever Von wants, you hook him up."

"Thanks, man."

"My treat." Howie leans closer, lowers his voice. "You just got out. You deserve to celebrate."

Now why couldn't Raul have had a similar attitude?

"That's great, Howie," Von says, lowering his voice. "But that favor I was talking about."

"Name it."

"Can you get me a burner?"

Howie straightens, frowning as he processes the request. The frown deepens, but he nods. "Sure, Von, no problem. Let me see what I can come up with."

"Cool."

"You gonna be here a while?"

Von's burger arrives with a heap of fries—their radiant heat warms his face. "I got all night."

Howie excuses himself, he's got to go get ready for the evening.

Tarzan's isn't a place you go to for food, generally speaking, but the burger tastes so good he has to remind himself not to eat like a just-released convict. The salty fries cause him to order another beer.

He holds this second glass, beading condensation, to his forehead. Between the long day under the hot sun and the lack of sleep, he feels like his brain is sizzling on a frying pan. Like one of those old anti-drug ads, and he hasn't even been doing any drugs.

The beer is sure going down easy, though.

He's disappointed in himself—he'd been committed to staying sober. But there are some days where only an ice-cold beer will do. Besides, a beer or two never hurt anybody.

The place is filling up now. Aside from the waitresses and dancers, the crowd is mostly men—he's surprised how young they all look. If he were carding, he'd throw half these guys out just on appearance alone. But then Howie wouldn't be making any money, now, would he? Nobody stays in business by turning away customers.

Von considers asking Howie if he has any clothes he can borrow. He knows he must look pretty ratty at this point, despite the tie, but he feels like that might be pushing his luck. Besides, even if they were more stylish, they would almost certainly hang unfashionably loose on Von's prison-reduced frame. Pastor Tom's shirt is snug, at least. Tight around the biceps. He snugs up the tie before tucking into the burger. Even though wearing a tie feels like a noose around his neck, in a place like Tarzan's it makes him look even more gangster. It's his look now.

A couple of guys—barely more than kids, reminding him of those high school parties—occupy the seats to his right.

Immediately the phones are out.

"Is Gonz coming?"

"Twenty minutes, he says."

"So, an hour and a half."

They bump fists with the bartender, though, so they must be regulars. One hands him a credit card to open a tab. The bartender returns with daiquiris. Which Von always thought of as a girly drink, but they look pretty damn good right about now, his belly full, his glass empty.

The bartender sweeps away his empty plate, asks if he wants another.

"I'll have what these gentlemen are having," he says.

The kid sitting next to him turns briefly toward him, acknowledges his existence at least. They're wearing polos with funky patterns, hair gelled to look like they just rolled out of bed.

"I couldn't help myself," Von says. "They look so damn tasty."

The kid raises his glass, turns toward his friend but also seems to be including Von in the toast, and says, "To Saturday night."

Von raises his glass, and clinks it against his neighbor's, and then his buddy's.

"Is it Saturday already?" Von asks.

This gets a laugh. "Hell yeah, bro! Fucking Saturday!"

"First Saturday since I got out."

"Out of where?" neighbor kid asks.

"*Out*, out," Von says, nudging his arm. "You know."

"No shit!" credit card kid says. "Dude, we gotta do shots."

"What did you do?" neighbor kid asks.

"Don't ask that!" his friend says.

"Killed a man," Von says. "In cold blood."

Credit card kid exhales the word "dude" for about three seconds. Von is genuinely concerned that neighbor kid might have pissed himself.

"I'm fucking with you," Von says. Both kids smile, breathe again. "Never ask a con what he did. Think about it—is a con ever gonna give you a straight answer?"

They both nod. Once again, Von is the old head. The sage, imparting his hard-earned wisdom to a couple of squares getting juiced before heading back to the lounge. Working up the courage to slip a bill into a dancer's g-string. To ask for a lap dance. To rub shoulders with some of the genuinely tough dudes who will start to trickle in eventually. This is kiddie hour. And he is Mr. Rogers. Welcome to Sesame Street.

Which are shows he only knows about because Shelly put them on for Tara. Because that was what she watched when she was a little girl, wide-eyed and innocent.

Let's not go there—not now.
What's this? A shot? Tequila?

"Here we go, boys," he says. He licks the base of his thumb, sprinkles salt over it. "We're in it, now."

"Making friends, Von?"

"Hey, Howie." Von stands, but his legs are stiff from all the walking and he has to steady himself on the stool. "Wanna join us?"

"Wish I could," Howie says, though he doesn't look all that eager.

"Boys, this is Howie. He owns the place." He claps his hand over Howie's heart. "Guy's got a heart as big as a Mack truck."

"Having a good time?" Howie shakes the boys' hands.

"Hells yeah," credit card kid says. If Von had a baggie of baking powder he could easily get a couple of bills out of this kid.

Except he'd want to pay with his credit card. Or his phone, or some shit.

"Here you go," Howie says, handing something to Von.

It's just a phone. An old Samsung with a spider web of cracks in the upper right corner.

He turns his back to the kids. "What's this?"

"I know it's cracked, but it works fine..."

"Howie." Von extends his pointer finger, cocks his thumb. "I meant a *burner*."

"Oh—shit, man. That's a whole other kettle of fish. What do you want that for?"

"Self-defense. It's a cold, cruel world out here."

"You can't just—"

"Buy one? I don't even have a permanent address yet."

Howie purses his lips, looks down at the tequila shot and the lime on the bar. The kids are waiting, shot glasses in one hand, limes in the other, for their newfound friend to join them.

"Can you handle it? Howard?"

"Uh, yeah. Yeah—sure. I got you."

"No serial numbers, right?" That should go without saying, of course, but Howie seems like he's shook.

"Let me make a few phone calls, see what I can do."

'See what I can do?' Has the whole world gone soft?

"Gracias, amigo."

"This is real short notice," Howie says.

Von pats Howie's heart again. "Do what you can. For auld lang syne, and all that shit."

Howie nods, and leaves them to it. Von turns back to the bar, lifts the lime and the shot glass.

"To Howie," he says. "A stand-up dude."

"To Howie!"

They slam their empty glasses down on the bar. "Wait till Gonz hears about this," credit card says in his friend's ear. The music is starting to whump and thump, and he says this louder than he wanted to, probably.

He's in the middle of a story when he is interrupted, not by Howie, but by a woman. Scantily clad, one of the dancers.

"Babe!" she squeals, forcing her way in between Von and neighbor kid.

Jasmine.

He barely recognizes her with all the makeup. Her hair is butched short now. And the passage of years, he supposes. Years without sparing her a second thought. She doesn't look bad, though.

"Howie said you were here," she says. "Weren't you going to come say hi?"

"I was getting there. But then I started telling these lads a story—"

"Did I interrupt?" The boys shake their heads, but Von says, "Yes."

"I'm sorry." She apologizes to the boys, then turns back to Von. "I just got so excited when I heard—"

He can see it in their eyes. To these kids, he has just gone from *gangster*, to *legend*. Just because chicks want to be with him—certain types anyway—that makes guys want to *be* him. Even the ones who suspected he was banging their girlfriends, even they looked up to him and were like, *God damn that dickhead—but how does he do it?*

He doesn't give a shit, that's how. He genuinely does not care if Jasmine is excited to see him. Sure, she's got a great pair of tits, and a nice ass. Credit where it's due. But who cares? He could've had her any time he wanted, back in the day—but he didn't want her.

Which only made her want him all the more. All these other clowns throwing their dicks at her, but who's the one guy she wants? The guy who looks dangerous, who doesn't say much, and who barely tolerates her presence.

Old Vonny boy.

"Ah, fuck it," Von says, with a wave of his hand. "I forgot what I was saying anyway."

"Don't be mad." She leans against his stool.

"Nobody's mad. When do you go on?"

"In fifteen."

"I'll come back and check it out."

"You better not! I'll be embarrassed."

"Please. You ain't been embarrassed since you were thirteen."

She smacks his shoulder playfully. "Asshole."

He winks over her shoulder at the lads, still his audience. Though now they're scooping their phones up from the bar. Credit card kid signals he's ready to close out. They're heading back to the lounge. Neighbor kid can't wait to get the hell out of there, but credit card kid makes a point of shaking Von's hand. He probably wants to ask Von if he has any of whatever it is he's into, but the kid is intimidated by Jasmine, who makes it clear she isn't going anywhere, now that she's found her man. Instead he says, "See you later?"

"I'm around," Von says. *Beat it, dork. The grown-ups are talking.*

"This is gonna sound crazy," Jasmine says. "Yesterday, I had my cards read, and Simone told me an important person from my past would come back into my life."

"Am I an important person?"

"Stop!" She nudges his thigh with her hip. Right where her short-short skirt stops and her fishnet thigh-highs begin. "You know I always had a thing for you. But you only had eyes for—what was her name?"

"Shelly," he says. The name dries his mouth. "What a mistake that was."

"What happened?"

"She couldn't wait for me."

"She couldn't even wait three years?"

"Four."

"What kind of woman can't wait four years for her man?"

"Hell, it's not that she couldn't wait for me to get out—she could barely wait for me to go in. I swear she had the paperwork ready, day one."

The paradox of women. The ones you don't give a shit about, they're the ones that won't leave you alone. But as soon as one knows she's got her hooks into you—soon as she knows you care—that's when she can't wait to get rid of you.

"For real?" Jasmine's eyes widen.

"She got what she wanted out of me," he says. He holds up three fingers up, folding them down one by one: "First the ring, then the kid, then the house. Guess she didn't need ol' Von no more."

"What a bitch," Jasmine says.

"Kinda makes you wonder, don't it? How I got sent up in the first place."

"No! Don't even say it—don't even think it!"

He shrugs. "She's all shacked up with a dude I thought was my bro. Best man at our wedding. Every job he ever had he got because of me. That's how the world repays you."

"You don't deserve to be treated like that," she says.

"Deserve ain't got nothing to do with it," he says.

She has leaned into him, her breast is pressing against his forearm.

"We should hang out sometime," she says.

"Yeah, sure," he says. "I'm still pretty shook, though."

She makes a frowny pout. "What about tonight?"

"I don't need nobody's pity." He shifts himself, forcing her to straighten. She tugs her skirt down her thighs.

"It's not pity."

"Have a seat." He points toward the vacated stool.

"You know I can't," she says. "Not when I'm working."

"Right."

"Come back and see me." Dragging her hand over his chest, then his shoulder, she turns and sashays away among the four-top tables crowded with lads hunched over pitchers and mugs and martini glasses, lifting their eyes to follow her twitching ass as she passes among them. He returns the envious stares of one or two of them, until their eyes drop.

He motions to the bartender, orders a Tully on the rocks. Too much of the sweet cocktails and he's gonna wake with a crushing headache. He reaches in his pocket to leave the guy a tip—between Howie and the kids, he hasn't paid for a thing—but then thinks better of it.

Twenty-two bucks won't get you very far these days.

He gets up and strides back toward the lounge, and all of a sudden the booze hits him. The strobing lights and the crushing sound are oppressive. Once in the lounge he picks his way among the tables until he finds a free chair, pulls it off to the side, and sinks down into it. He needs to nurse this round, but looks down to find that it's mostly gone, and he's not sure if he drank it all, or spilled some of it while wrestling with the chair.

Saturday night. Fuckin-A right.

He can't even tell who's up on stage, with the lights. Maybe it's Jasmine, maybe it's not. He never really did find the dancing—these cheerleader routines, spinning round a flagpole—all that interesting.

A hand taps his shoulder, and he knows he's been zoning out. Probably a bouncer, telling him he's had enough, time to call it a night.

But it's Howie, reaching over the railing. Motioning for him to follow.

He's awake now. Alert. *Go time. Game face.* He vaults the railing. Howie leads him back to the bathrooms.

The stalls are unisex, men and women share the sinks. You

might think a place like Tarzan's wouldn't draw a lot of women, but you'd be surprised. Where else are you going to find a bunch of horny young dudes, like credit card kid and wimpy wingman, out on the town, ripe for the honey pot? Von and Howie pass behind a couple of hotties reapplying lipstick, touching up their hair. Von nods at their haughty reflections in the mirror. Sharks know where to swim. Game respects game.

He and Howie squeeze into a stall. From another stall comes a strong snorted inhale, followed by an outrushing strangulated roar. Howie pulls a little .38 revolver from his pants pocket, hands it to Von. It is deceptively weighty, the curvaceous knurled handle rough to the touch. He swings out the cylinder—unloaded—snaps it back into place.

"How much?" Von asks.

"Don't worry about it," Howie says. "I got you."

"You know that ain't how I roll—but I ain't in a position to make a stink. Gimme a few days, and I'll pay you back."

"I know you're good for it, Von."

"You're a class act, Howie. I know you're bending over backward for me here."

"You're not going to do anything stupid, right?" Howie asks. "I mean, you just got out."

"What—now you're going to lecture me, too?"

"All right," Howie lifts his now empty hands. "How many rounds you need?"

Back out in the lounge, the music is louder, if that is even possible. The ballers are starting to roll in, splashing real cash, claiming their turf, clearing out the kiddos. If he doesn't have another drink, the tightness in his temples is going to bend into something sinister. But the bartender here doesn't know him from Adam, and Howie is nowhere to be seen. Jasmine, on the other hand, is being kept busy giving lap dances to some professional-looking Indian dude. The goofy smile plastered on his face says he's probably on molly, or something similar. He keeps getting handsy with her, until a bouncer gets in his face, and then he cools it, chastised. Afraid he's going to get kicked out, and separated from his crush.

Von catches her eye as she's coming out of one of the private suites. Motions with his head toward the bar. When she reaches him there, sweat is showing through her caked-on makeup, and she's breathing heavy.

"What's up?" she says. "I can't be on break yet."

"Who's the clown?" he asks.

"Why?" she asks. Then smiles. "Jealous?"

"Maybe," he lies. "Trying to get a rise out of me?"

"Maybe," she says.

"Well?"

"He's just some guy."

"He a regular?"

She nods. "Off and on."

"You and him doing the dirty?"

She leans into him, and he can smell her sweat. Or maybe it's his own, that she's blowing back to him.

"Not when I got something better going on." She runs her hand down his tie, then wraps her hand around the dangling silk and pulls him toward her with it.

"You like the tie, don't you? Maybe I'll get a chance to use it on you later."

She leans in toward him, brushes her lips against his ear, whispers, "I'd like that."

"You remember the game we used to run on these clowns?"

She drops her hand from his tie. "I remember how we used to celebrate after."

"You up for bringing it back?" he asks. "Up for running a little game?"

"I'm up for celebrating your freedom. Just you and me."

"How about we include this guy in our little game. That's part of the fun."

She steps back, her face clouding. "Those were dark times for me, Von. I used to get so stressed. Gave me an ulcer."

"It'll be quick—"

"No, Von," she says. "I'm not doing that anymore. I can't."

"Jasmine."

"I'm not that person anymore."

He studies her face, sees the resolve. He knows where she likes to take these guys. The ones who can't take her back to their homes, where they live with their wives, and their kids.

"I ain't asking you to do anything you wouldn't be doing anyway. Just hang out with him somewhere. That spot on the beach, right? Where it's quiet?"

She shakes her head. "Von, I—"

"Just this once," he says. "For old times."

She's quiet, then looks around, as though startled to remember where she is.

"What kind of car does he drive?"

"Mercedes S-Class. Black."

"What is he, a doctor?"

"Engineer," she says, with a little sigh. "I think. I have to get back to work."

"Go do your thing," he says. "Play nice."

When she leaves, he orders a rum and coke. A bit of booze, a bit of caffeine. A pick-me-up. Can't leave right after talking to her—too obvious. There are eyes everywhere, making digital recordings from every angle. Besides, he still has some time to kill. He can make it there in an hour—assuming the bike is still where he left it.

His drink arrives, and he pays for it from his very limited supply. Leaving himself with a grand total of seven dollars. Hopefully, by the end of the night, that number will be substantially augmented.

Good thing he's still got some friends, out here in the suck. Otherwise he'd really be screwed.

CHAPTER
EIGHT

HIS BIKE IS STILL behind the dumpster where he left it, and now he's cruising along Vanderbilt, the balls of his bare feet pushing the pedals, with the pastor's too-tight shoes laced together and dangling from his neck, one on either side, bouncing against his chest.

He crosses one bridge, then another, out onto the island. The gulf breeze cools the sweat from his brow, lifts the shirt from his back. But the headwind also forces him to pedal harder, tiring his legs.

Then he spots the Mercedes. Parked at the far end of an empty lot, next to one of the omni-present green metal dumpsters, facing the beach and the ocean. Perfect—that'll give him some cover from cars passing on the road. There shouldn't be many, though, at this hour, even on a Saturday night.

He passes the car, continues on for a minute or so, then wheels the bike into the shadow of yet another ruined beach house, moonlight bleaching its silent skeleton. He hops down, his crotch sore, and props the bike against one of several concrete pillars supporting a hollow shell above, nothing left but floors and walls, everything else washed away by winds and surging floodwaters.

He was a big fan of Ian, when it tore through. Watched its progress on the news every chance he got. Gleefully chortled at the images of all these rich assholes losing their beachfront vacation palaces, then having the gall to moan about it on TV.

This is what the world needs. He waves filthy strands of dangling insulation out of his face. *Another Ian, but a hundred times over. Flatten the place. Level the playing field. That's the only way anything is ever going to truly change.*

Don't you see, Nature? You might wreck shit here, wreak some havoc there—but that's not how you get respect. Not from people. Come on—do you even know us? You raised us, bitch. We're your children. You should know by now that if you want to get your point across—if you want our respect—you gotta push back HARD.

He laces up the preacher's shoes and walks back along the sidewalk. He waits till there are no cars coming in either direction, then quickly steps to the dumpster, moves around to the ocean side of it, sits in the shallow layer of white sand blown up from the beach. He doesn't hear any noises from the car over the gentle waves and the steady breeze.

He sits in the cool breeze sweeping in from the gulf. He tries one of the breathing exercises Mr. Counselor Dude showed him. In for four, hold for four, out for four, wait for four. Repeat. Regulate the nervous system. Slow the heartbeat.

Easier said than done.

Sounds from the car disturb his meditation. Murmurings. A low voice, insistent. A higher pitched voice, whining. Pleading.

He crawls into the gap between the car and the dumpster, into the shadow cast by the moon. Leans his back against the rear tire, passenger side. He presses his ear against the tiny crack where the door meets the wheel well.

He's begging now.

He gives them a little more time. To make sure he catches him with his pants down. At his most vulnerable.

She's gone silent. He's more assertive. Not just louder—closer. Maybe they're both in the passenger seat?

Silence.

Then, a grunt. Another. Another. Now he's getting in there.

She begins to punctuate his grunts with her own.

"Oh, baby," he says.

Baby. Von stifles a chuckle. *Please. This is how guys like you get got.*

He doesn't feel bad for what he's about to do to this guy: dude brought it on himself.

This is the problem with most guys, he thinks. *They want so bad to believe that this chick is into them, they let themselves get carried off into this fantasy land. Later, they'll blame her, of course, but if they're being honest, they'd have to admit they played themselves.*

I mean, listen to yourself, dude—you're completely out of control. And it might sound like she is too, like she's even enjoying it. Oh, yeah—you're really giving it to her now, pal. She's about to come, any second now. Sure. You're all caught up in this image of yourself as a god, just because you're getting your dick wet—meanwhile, far as she's concerned, it's all an act.

She's a stripper, dude. This is what she does. She puts on a show. And you're a fool, thinking you mean something to her.

He pulls the revolver from his pants pocket. He's never been super comfortable with guns. But a gun is a tool, like any other. A tool for shaping human behavior.

She's fucking you, pal, but she's thinking about me,

wondering where I am. She's willing to fuck you—and feel absolutely nothing—if she thinks that will get her what she wants.

And you, my friend, have no idea what's about to happen to you.

He stands, gun in his right, pulls at the passenger door handle with his left.

Open. *Beautiful.*

An explosion of sound and movement in the cabin, leaving Jasmine splayed, skirt hiked above her hips, in the reclined passenger seat. The clown has thrown himself toward the other side of the car, but the shift and the steering wheel have obstructed him.

"No you don't." Von grabs his pants, down around his shins, and drags him toward him.

Jasmine bends her knees and lifts her legs out from under the guy. Exposing her bare ass, reddened in the faint moonlight. She's screaming, but not too loud. Not louder than the dude is.

"Shut up!" Von smashes the gun barrel into the guy's junk, then again. When he reaches down to protect himself, Von leans back and digs his heels into the concrete to haul him from the car.

He has him halfway out when the preacher's smooth-soled shoes slip on the sandy surface, and Von goes down on his own ass. Hard. He releases his grip, and the guy is scrambling to get back inside, reaching behind to close the door.

If that happens, and he locks the door, it's game over.

Von puts his foot in the door frame, and the door bounces off it. He doesn't even feel it—but he knows he will. As it swings back toward him, he catches the door in his left and pulls himself forward, still sitting, but now fully in the path of the door. He aims the gun squarely at the guy's face: he is cowering in the space between the glove compartment and the passenger seat.

"I will fucking end you, bro," Von says.

He raises his hands.

Von gets his feet under him. Putting weight on his left sends blinding flashes of light shooting up into his eyes. He wonders if any bones are broken.

"Get out here," he says, through gritted teeth. He grabs the guy by his hair, and drags him out of the car, forcing him down and scrambling on hands and knees.

"You too!" he yells at Jasmine. "What are you waiting for?"

She steps out, pulls her skirt down.

He waves the gun in her direction, and she screams, lifts her hands.

"Get down!" he yells. "On the ground! You wanna get shot?"

Left hand still clutching a hank of the guy's hair, Von buries the barrel into the nape of his neck, and drags him around the passenger door, to the beach side of the dumpster —better cover from the road. He can't be sure whether any cars have driven by in the few seconds that have passed, but he thinks they're probably okay.

Still—let's make this quick. Wrap this up.

"Nice night for a little fuckie-suckie." He stands behind the guy, bends down over him so he can talk directly into his ear. "Gimme your wallet, asshole."

The guy's pants are still down around his ankles, and he tries to reach back for them.

"Never mind," he says. "Don't move."

He finds the wallet in one pocket, the keys in another. The man's ass is glowing brightly in the moonlight.

"Take the cash and cards," he whimpers. "But please, sir. Please leave my ID."

Pleading to a different tune now, aren't we?

Von's mouth is back at the guy's ear. "I'll take what I want, dumb-ass. In fact, I'll take your life if you say another fucking word."

"Leave us alone!" Jasmine says. *Good job*, he thinks. *Keeping up the act.*

"Tell your bitch to shut up," Von instructs the man. "Or I'ma put a bullet in your brain."

Beneath his grip on his hair, the man's head turns toward Jasmine.

"Tell her, man!"

"Shut up," the man says. "Please."

"Not like that," Von says. "Tell her 'shut up, bitch.'"

"What?"

"You got a hearing problem? Say 'what' one more time. I dare you!"

"Shut up... bitch. Please."

"Good Lord—you goddamn simp. Can't even say that right."

He straightens and opens the wallet. It's stuffed full of small bills—ready for a night at Tarzan's. But there's at least a hundred in there, maybe even two once he has a chance to count.

He searches the man's remaining pockets. Empty.

"Keys."

"Come on, man—"

"Where are the keys?"

"They're in the car."

"This one of them cars where you don't have to put the key in the ignition?"

The man's head shifts beneath his hand, nodding.

"Fancy," he says. "Well, I'm going to take it, and I'm going to take your bitch here. And I'm going to put my key in her ignition."

"Please, mister," she whines.

"Better tell her to shut up and go along with me, bro." He tightens his grip, burrows the barrel into the man's neck.

"No, don't," she says.

"Tell her, bro."

"Best to do what he says," the poor guy says.

"You heard your man," Von says.

He yanks the man's pants down over his ankles. Tosses them out over the sand. Shoves the man over onto his side. He grabs Jasmine by the hair and hauls her to her feet.

She screams. "Leave me alone!" Too loud.

He smacks her—with the hand holding the pistol.

"Shut up," he says.

"Please, sir," the man says, from the sand.

"Are you insane?" Von stalks toward him, aiming the gun at the man's head, dragging Jasmine along behind, whimpering. "You got some sort of a death wish, bro?"

The man turns his head away.

Will he recognize me from the bar? Von wonders. *I oughta make sure...*

He straightens. Looks at the half-moon, lowering out over the gulf. The waves roll in, then wash back.

Sucker only had eyes for Jasmine. He wasn't noticing anything or anybody else.

Von squats by the guy's head, forcing Jasmine down to her knees in the sand at his side. The gun dangles over his right knee, and the guy groans and cranes his neck, looking away.

"You think you're a smart guy?" he asks, voice calm. Rational. "Trying to memorize my face so you can rat me out to the cops later?"

"No, please sir. I swear—"

"Bury your head in the sand," Von says. *Poetic justice. That's how you got yourself in this little predicament in the first place.*

The man nods, eyes closed. He inhales as though he's about to dunk his head under water, and presses his face into the sand.

"Come on, bitch," Von says, as he stands.

He almost doesn't make it upright. His foot is beginning to throb.

He leads Jasmine around to the passenger door. She is begging him not to, begging him to leave her alone, please, no, stop, don't do this, you're hurting me, all the right words. Once in, he slams the door closed, then skips around the front to the driver side, the gun trained at the passenger seat the whole time in case the guy is watching. When he reaches the driver side, it is locked, and he raps softly on the window for Jasmine to open. The guy is still lying on his side, shoulders and head hidden by the dumpster, underwear wrapped around his shoes.

The door opens, and he is in. He sits, and sets the gun on the floor at his feet. He finds the ignition switch, and the engine roars to life. He reverses, turns, then guns it, spitting sand, out onto the road.

He turns to Jasmine. Her head is in her hands. She is sobbing.

"It's okay," he says. "You can drop the act."

She doesn't move, aside from her shoulders, which keep shaking.

His right hand is trembling from all the adrenaline coursing through his body as he reaches to pull her left hand down and away from her face.

There is blood. On her cheek, on her forehead, on her hand.

"Oh, shit," he says. "Did I get you, babe?"

She nods, whimpers, sniffles.

"Fuck," he says. "I was only trying to make it look realistic, you know?"

He releases her hand, and she returns it to her face.

"Ow," she says. "You fucked up my face, Von."

"Maybe he's got some napkins, in the glove compartment. You need to apply some pressure."

"I can't move!" she says. "I'm bleeding everywhere!"

He pulls over to the side of the road, opens the glove compartment. Finds a packet of sanitary wipes.

No gun, he thinks, with a shake of his head—*but at least you're safe from germs.*

"Use these," he says. He drops the pack in her lap.

"That's gonna sting," she whines.

"No shit," he says, as he puts the car in gear and guns it forward again. "But it'll keep it from getting infected."

She doesn't move.

"You don't want it to get infected, do you?"

She shakes her head.

"Have to go to the hospital? Get plastic surgery?"

She pulls one of the wipes from the plastic wrapper, wipes her hands with it, smearing it pink. She pulls out another one, and dabs it to her forehead.

"Ow," she moans. "Ow, ow, ow! Fuck, Von. Fucking hell. Why'd you bring me along with you? Now they're going to think I'm in on it!"

"No they won't," he says. "Not with a shiner like that."

"This isn't a shiner, Von!"

"Well." He coughs. "Not yet."

"How am I supposed to go to work with my face all fucked up?"

"That's why God invented makeup," he says. He knows he's being an asshole right now, but he can't help himself. He's so wired. So freaking *amped*.

Breathe. You did it—it's over. Take your foot off the gas.

They slow from a hundred, to eighty, to sixty, to forty. The speed limit is thirty-five.

Last thing you need is a speeding ticket.

"Look at it this way," he says. "At least I already hit you. I was going to have to do that at some point, no matter what, so they wouldn't suspect you. At least now it's done."

"Great," she says. "Wonderful."

"And now you're not stuck on the beach with that clown, trying to come up with some story."

"You think I'm worried about *him*, Von? I'm worried about the fucking cops."

"I'll put you out down at the bridge," he says. "Call the cops from there."

"There's nothing there, Von."

"What do you mean?"

"It's all gone. Ian wrecked it all."

"Surely there's *something* there." This was the tourist hub of Fort Myers Beach, a neon and dayglo encrustation of tiki bars and T-shirt shops right at the foot of the bridge leading to the mainland.

She lowers her head to her knees. "This night is going to suck, isn't it?" Her voice is soft. Exhausted. Defeated.

He reaches out, places his hand on the back of her neck. She tenses, then relents. "I'll make it up to you," he says.

"You better," she says. She sits up straight, and he returns his hand to the wheel. The throbbing in his left foot has built into a steady pulsation of pain.

He rolls down his window. The cool sea breeze floods the car, cools his brow, and the arm that he leans on the sill.

"You sure waited long enough," she says. She has dropped her hands from her face, and is leaning her forehead against the darkened passenger-side window.

"You seemed to be enjoying yourself," he says. He pats her left hip.

She *tsks*, scoots even further away from him.

"Well, I wasn't," she says. "I thought you weren't coming."

"I said I'd be there," he says. "It took me a minute to find you."

Silence.

"I found you, though. Didn't I?"

He pulls to the side of the road in front of a little motel near the base of the bridge. Jasmine was right, there is hardly anything left down here. One good thing about that: no surveillance cameras. The neon flamingo above the door is lit up; within a young man sits at the desk, staring at his phone. Von rolls the Mercedes further down, so they won't draw the kid's attention when she gets out of the car.

"I don't have your address," he says. "I need a place to crash."

"What, my place?" she asks. "Oh, no. That doesn't—"

"Come on, babe," he says. "Just for tonight. Don't you want to see me?"

"Of course I do," she says.

"I thought you were happy to see me."

"I am."

She turns in her seat to face him. "You're not going to rip me off, are you, Von?"

He has parked under an orange street light, and in the dim glow filtering through the tinted windshield the right side of her face is grotesque, her makeup streaked, the corner of her mouth turned down. The left side is hidden in shadow, and that is probably for the best.

"Of course not," he says. That's why we took down this clown. I got all I need for now."

"Please don't dick me over, Von," she says. "My heart couldn't take it."

"Don't you trust me?"

She turns, and stares forward through the windshield, bites her lower lip. Heaves a dramatic sigh.

What can she possibly be looking at out there? Ruins. Empty lots. Darkness.

"I do, Von, though why... I honestly have no idea."

She turns to him, and smiles, faintly.

"I guess I'm just a hopeless romantic."

"Oh, yeah?" he says. "How romantic?"

"Jesus, Von." She slaps his shoulder.

"What?" he says. "Your boy's been in the clink for four years!"

"Here?" she says. "Now?"

"Just some head."

He unbuttons and unzips, pulls himself free. He's not hard, but he's getting there.

"You're making this up to me," she says.

"Soon as I get this shit sorted with custody and visitations," he says, "we're getting the hell out of Dodge. I'm taking you far away from here."

She purses her lips, but she takes him in her right hand, places her left on his thigh, leans over him.

"I just got so worked up," he says. He moans involuntarily as she wraps her lips around him. "Listening to you guys going at it. And then taking that guy down. Did you see how scared he was?"

Does he mean it? The bit about taking her far away, with him? Maybe if he had a woman in the picture, that would help with custody. With the courts.

Who are you kidding? She's a chick that goes down on a guy like you, in a car he just stole, from a guy she was just fucking. How's that going to help your case?

The real question is—did you mean it when you told the mark you were going to put a bullet in his brain?

Because, for a second there, you were close. And it wasn't even in the heat of the moment. It was a calculated decision. You made the right call—but still...

If it had been Darnell... or Raul... or even Shelly...
Maybe then. Maybe there will come a time.

His foot is pulsing now, almost in time with the bobbing of Jasmine's head. It's killing the vibe.

She lifts up, draws in breath. Glances up toward him, saliva stringing from her mouth. The gash he's given her at her temple is garish in the streetlight: drying blood still glistening, purple swelling nearly forcing her eye closed.

"You close?" she pants.

He places his hand on her shoulder and gently pushes her back.

"I want to—" she says. "I was just wondering—"

"Your face," he says, as he zips up. "It's kinda distracting."

She sits up straight, as though he'd slapped her all over again. "Thanks a lot."

"What?" he says. "I know it's my fault. I said I'll make it up to you."

She sighs, slumps back into the seat. She doesn't want to leave, he can tell.

"What am I going to say?" she asks.

"Say I tried to force myself on you, and you fought me off, and then I hit you and kicked you out of the car. Tell them what I look like—they're going to get that from your boyfriend anyway. Just say that you've never seen me before, you have no idea who I am. I'll deal with the heat when it comes."

"I guess I should go," she says.

"What about your address?"

"Oh, yeah." She tells him. The door closes behind her, and he watches her walk around the front of the car, and limp into the lobby of the motel. He can't tell if the limp is real, or fake. She's good, he has to hand it to her.

He pulls away.

He's got a car, now, and some cash—he'll have to total it

up when he gets to a safe place, where he can search the car thoroughly.

But I didn't get my rocks off, AND I had to hit a woman? What a shitty night.

At least I didn't hit her BECAUSE she didn't get me off.

At least I ain't that kind of guy.

CHAPTER
NINE

THE BOOZE and the adrenaline have drained from his system, leaving him with the pain in his left foot. This is countered, however, by a great deal of pleasure thrumming through his right foot: *he is driving*. Forget sex—it's been four years since he last drove a car, down empty highways, late at night, windows down, bugging out. When is a man more *alive* than in moments like these, fused with a powerful machine that responds to his slightest touch? He doesn't even have any music on—couldn't figure out how to get the radio to play, what with all the touchscreen nonsense—but that's okay. He'd rather be alone with his thoughts. Or with the rush of wind washing his thoughts away.

And here he is. Coasting to a stop in front of his house. He'd put the system on cruise control, and this is where his good foot brought him.

He had an idea this was where he'd wind up.

He reaches down between his legs, finds the .38. So ugly, this strange mix of shapes: short barrel, fat cylinder, curved handle. Compared to a nine, it looks like something a kindergartener designed. But it fits snug in his hand.

Tara. She's the sticking point. The knife in his ribs. The throbbing in his foot.

She was so *grown*.

So much I missed out on. Because of these dime-dropping back-stabbers.

She's what keeps him from going in there right now and finding those two traitors and emptying the gun into them. Sleeping in his bed. Fucking in his bed. Although, let's be real, now that Shelly's got him, she probably ain't fucking him, either. He knows how that story goes. Been there, done that, got the T-shirt.

They didn't even have the decency to find a new place. That right there is a total lack of respect.

No one will say or do anything to you that you don't invite them to do. Had to talk that one through with Mr. Counselor Dude after the other guys had cleared out so he wouldn't seem tryhard. Once it clicked, though—*bro*. Total mind-fuck, to realize he'd been the one inviting all this shitty treatment, all these years.

Well, he ain't putting out that invitation no more, no how. No sir.

He's got money, he's got wheels, he's got a gun. Maybe most important, he's got the element of surprise on his side. Now is when he should act. A preemptive strike. Before they get some sense, and move out.

You're being impulsive again, he thinks.

If he were to shoot Darnell, and Shelly, even if he managed to get away, what would happen to Tara? Shelly's parents won't take her: they practically disowned her from the moment she introduced them to Von. One look at him and their minds were made up. Not good enough for their precious Shelly.

A ward of the state. That's what she would become.

How could he put her through that?

He was eighteen when his mom died, and he's had to fend for himself from then on. From before then—ever since she got sick, when he was sixteen. But still—he was a teenager, at least. Knew how to navigate the world.

But six, he considers. *You can't do anything for yourself. You don't know anything about how the world really works. You're innocent.*

Innocence took one look at me, and wanted nothing to do with me.

Probably for the best.

He can't even remember what she looks like. All he got was a glimpse before she buried her face in her mother's legs. His very presence making her cry.

He gets out of the car.

He still has this image in his mind of her as a little toddler, eyes bright, wobbling from the coffee table to his knee and back again. He just wants to see her one more time, and then he'll leave her alone. Doesn't want her to see him—he knows that would scare her. But maybe, through the window...

The blinds are down. He touches his fingertips to the glass.

Tara. My beautiful baby girl.

He's even tearing up. He's exhausted. His foot is killing him. He's drunk, or at least he was—and booze always makes him maudlin by the end of the night.

Unless it makes him belligerent.

He hobbles around the corner of the house. Past the humming AC unit in Tara's room. The next window is his old bedroom's window. The blinds are down here, too—and that's a good thing. If he were to actually see them sleeping next to each other, in what used to be his bed, he'd probably shoot them both right then and there.

His left foot swings into a tricycle and a bolt of pain straightens his spine, closes his eyes, opens his mouth—he jams his fist into his teeth to stifle the shout, bites down on his knuckles.

He stumbles into the backyard. A motion-detecting light clicks on. *That's new.* He staggers toward the wall, leans his back into the rough stucco. Their AC unit hums loudly. He waits an eternity for the light to switch off.

He crouches, hugs the wall, creeps in stealth mode to the screened-in, astroturfed patio. Eases open the flimsy screen door.

Why, dude? What's the point?

Remember what you said to Pastor Tom: "I ain't about revenge—I'm all about respect."

Right—that's the point. Dude is sleeping in MY house. With MY woman. Even if she is a betraying back-stabber.

With MY daughter.

She's the knife in my side.

She's the one who makes me want to storm in there and take her away. Even if she did reject me.

But she's also the one that makes me think, no, this isn't the right way to go about it.

So maybe he has to spare Shelly.

But Darnell. The betrayal. It's eating away at me. He set me up. He got me sent away to get me out of the picture. And now he's trying to replace me, to be dad to my daughter.

I can't just let that shit stand.

The door is locked. No surprise. Around front, though—there are glass panes to either side of the door. He'd said something to the landlord about how that didn't seem very safe, when they first moved in, but the guy just shrugged. Take it or leave it, pal.

They think they've got all the time in the world. They think I'm just going to bend over and take it.

He should know me better than that. That's how you know we were never truly friends—if we were, he would've known to get his ass long gone by now. Across the country, because I will track your ass down. Best believe.

The front door is locked as well. He reverses his grip on the gun, barrel and cylinder in his grasp, raps the butt against the pane beside the doorknob. Harsh tinkle of brittle glass.

He holds his breath. Nothing. Silence. Darkness. A hush hangs over the neighborhood. The sky is brightening beyond the rooftops, out over the Everglades.

He shifts the gun to his left hand, reaches inside with his right, feels for the doorknob's little flat nipple—

He hears the movement—a swish, a grunt. He tries to pull out, but something snaps down around his wrist like a bear trap. Sharp and decisive. Permanent.

He hauls his hand free, half expecting to see a bloody stump. His hand is still there—*thank you, Lord*—but hanging limp, at a fucked-up angle.

A dagger of glass from the broken pane hangs from the soft tissue inside his wrist. He pulls it free, and the gap it leaves behind wells up red, starts to spill over with blood.

He drops the shard and staggers down the stoop, cradling his wrist. He can't stop himself from howling now—*motherfucker*, over and over.

He inspects his hand, his wrist, his forearm. Blood running down to his elbow now, darkening the white cloth of his rolled-up shirt sleeve. A strange lump protrudes from his wrist, like an extra bone. Hesitantly—tentatively—he rotates his hand, against the pain. It turns. It's not broken.

Must've been a blunt object. A baseball bat. A crowbar.

Motherfucker. Ain't that just like you, you sneaky little pussy, to cower in ambush like that.

From within, a man's panicked voice, "Go away!"

Doesn't sound like Darnell—but who else could it be?

He shifts the gun back to his right hand. Turns and strides back toward the door. Raises the gun. Squeezing the trigger sends a bolt of pain through his arm, into his jawbone.

But he fights through the pain, through the kick. Fights through the trigger's slippery elusiveness, blood coating it like baby lotion. Pulls that trigger again, one pull with each determined step. Once, twice, thrice. Aiming at the broken pane. At the doorknob. At the door. Striding forward like the goddamn Terminator. Relentless. Keeps pulling until the hammer is clicking.

A man grunts; a heavy weight crashes to the floor.

Click-click-click. The cylinder keeps turning.

A light comes on, and Von sees the upper body of the man through the broken pane.

A black man. Though his complexion seems lighter than Darnell's, his hair bushier. Maybe that's just a trick of the light.

A woman screams.

The man sprawled on the floor—she throws herself down next to him, lifts his head, cradles him. Her body now hides the man's face from Von.

But one thing is certain—she is also black.

She is not Shelly.

He reads the number on the door. Surveys the mangy yard that he crossed less than forty-eight hours ago. Reads the number on the door again.

Yep—this is his house.

Right place.

Wrong time.

Time to go.

He sprints for the car. His bloody fingers—still wrapped around the gun—smear the door handle, slip on the ignition button. The machine roars to life beneath his touch, and he turns across the road, bounces up onto the facing property's sidewalk, scraping their fake white plastic picket fence before skipping back down into the street.

He races away, foot pounding, wrist throbbing, right hand slipping down from the steering wheel to lay senselessly in his lap, still clutching the empty revolver. He wants to rid himself of it, but the pain is so great that he can't even bring himself to raise his arm.

He is trembling. He is exhausted. He is parched. He is in so much pain. He doesn't know if he's ever been in this much pain.

It's all gone to shit, he thinks. *Just like you knew it would.*

Negative self-talk, he admonishes himself. *Not helping anybody.*

Right. Keep it together. Find someplace to ditch the car, then the gun.

But where?

He finds himself driving toward the beach. Toward the water. Maybe he can ditch the car there, walk into the surf, let the gulf swallow him whole. End this before it gets any worse.

Even as he thinks it, he knows he won't do it. He's a survivor. That's what he does—he survives.

"Somehow, some way"—he nods along to his own sermon —"I'm going to get out of this."

Bro—you just shot an innocent man. Maybe even killed him.

"I just need to think," he says. "I need a plan. Gotta be smarter."

All because you were so goddamn sure it was Darnell behind that door. So sure. So righteous.

Mr. Counselor Dude is riding along beside him. His face is set in grim resignation. He can't even bring himself to turn toward Von. "Actions have consequences," he says, tired of having to repeat himself so many times. "Our choices have consequences."

"I know!" Von pounds the steering wheel with the gun. Winces at the pain that shoots up his arm.

"It should've been him!" he yells.

CHAPTER
TEN

HE IS surprised to see cars in the church parking lot.

Saturday night—an image of the two dorks at Tarzan's, gawking at him and Jasmine, doing shots because "it's Saturday night!"—*leads to Sunday morning*.

He parks among the cars, safe for now. Hidden among the herd. He'll move it to the grass behind the dumpster once people are gone. To hide it from the road. Plenty of time to give it a thorough search later, total up the take. Right now he just needs to clean himself up—lick his wounds—and crash.

Another car enters the parking lot, then another.

So even though their church is all gone to shit, people are still coming here? To hear this crazy old coot?

And you thought your life was fucked.

He reaches for the wipes. To clean up his arm at least.

What a mess. He's not the squeamish type, but all the blood—drying along his bare forearm, darkening the rolled-up shirt cuff, staining his pants—is making him queasy. Dizzy, even.

He snaps awake. Moments later, or maybe minutes.

An elderly couple is staring at him, through the car's open window.

Shit, I fell asleep. Or passed out.

He nods at them, smiles. Waves with his left.

"Go ahead on in," he says. "Just gathering my thoughts."

They both frown, the man tries to lead the woman away and she resists for a moment—as though she might be able to help this poor boy somehow—but her wiser half insists and they turn away and continue on toward the church, clucking and shaking their heads. He rolls up the tinted window, then kills the engine, as they disappear around the side of the building.

He wipes at the blood on his arm. Tentatively dabs at the cut itself.

Oh, Lord. This wakes him up. This is a different kind of pain, a much higher-pitched stinging that blinds him, and won't go away.

Fuck it, he thinks. *If Jasmine can do it and not be a bitch about it—*

He clamps a fresh wipe down over the wound, and holds it there. Applies pressure. Even scrubs a bit.

He's cursing now. Taking the good Lord's name in vain, and on a Sunday morning, in a church's parking lot, with old folks flocking in.

Oh, well. He laughs. *Going to hell anyway, ain't I? No matter what I do.*

Might as well enjoy the ride.

He wipes the worst of the blood from the steering wheel, the door handles. Not perfect, but it'll do. He tucks the crimson wad of wipes under the driver's seat. Locates the clown's keys amid a clutter of charging cables and chewing gum and breath mints and coffee cups. He exits the car, locks the door, and weaves his way through the cars—there are maybe twenty.

Crap cars, too—not the sort you see cruising into Bay Mar Estates. Hyundais and Nissans, Chevys and Fords. The wooziness unsteadies him, and he catches himself on a car's trunk, leans there for a moment, blinking and shaking his head.

The car's logo catches his eye. *A Saturn? Who still drives a Saturn?*

He pushes himself upright. The heel of his hand leaves a dark U-shaped smudge smiling back at him from faded blue paint. He dips his left index finger into fresh blood. Paints one eye above the ragged grin, then another.

Have a nice day!

Von rounds the corner, and stops short.

Church is outside today. The congregation is sitting on white folding chairs, arrayed in rows on the lawn. Their backs are to him; Pastor Tom stands at the front, facing him. At least he's wearing a shirt today, and pants.

Von props himself against the wall. The building's stucco digs into his palm. Probably leaving a fucked-up smile there, too.

He's sorely tempted to just lay himself down in the crabgrass at his feet and have a nap right then and there.

Can't do that. Someone will notice, and make a fuss. Call an ambulance. Which will get the police involved.

Come on, bro—you can make it. Ain't nobody tougher than you.

Crossing the fifty feet or so from the wall to the trailer is like walking a tightrope. He focuses on the door. Doesn't dare glance to either side.

Even though it feels like Pastor Tom's eyes are burning through the back of his skull.

Even though it feels like church has ground to a record-scratching halt, and all of the graybeards and whitehairs are turning in their seats to watch this strange pilgrim's progress.

Then he's there. Beneath the awning. The door is

unlocked. He lifts his right foot to the lower step, leans into it —fine. But his right hand slips off the door's handle, and it swings closed on him. He collapses forward onto the steps. Hauls himself up and in with his good hand, pushing with his good foot. The door softly clicks shut behind him.

That could've gone smoother.

He strips out of his bloody clothes—they're his now: *you bleed on it, you bought it*. He'll buy Pastor Tom a nice new suit. Monday, first thing. Well, maybe not a *nice* new suit. Suits are expensive. Second-hand. Good as new. It's the least he can do.

Literally, the least. That's your MO, your entire life.
Stop that. Stay positive.

Getting his left foot out of Pastor Tom's shoe is a struggle. His foot has swollen against the already-tight and rather unforgiving leather. Probably not even real leather. A couple of his toenails are blackened.

In the bathroom, he cracks open the little frosted window. The strains of the geezer choir in full voice filter in, accompanying him while he waits until steam from the shower fills the tiny cubby. He stands beneath the hot blast. Water and soap wash away the blood, and the grime, and the sweat.

Not the sin, though.
Can't wash that away.

The cut on his wrist starts bleeding again, and burning with the soapy water, but it's a good sign that it had just about stopped on its own. It's not that deep, now that he inspects it. He's got an enormous purple goose-egg growing out of his wrist, and it prevents him from flexing very far, but it's not broken. Same with his foot. It's not pleasant, but he can put weight on it.

He dries off, wraps the towel around his waist. In the kitchen he finds paper towels, wraps several around his wrist, then takes the kitchen towel and loops that around those, knots it into place. A better bandage than he would've gotten in the hospital.

His shorts and hoodie are folded neatly on the bench where he slept. He pulls these on, careful not to dislodge the bandage.

In the freezer he finds a package of frozen peas. He sits down on the bench, and covers the bruise on top of his foot with the peas, then wraps the wet shower towel around his foot to hold it in place. Stretches himself out, on his side, facing the back of the bench, away from the trailer door.

Outside, the singing continues.

Glory to God in the highest.
Glory, glory, glory.
Amen, brother. Amen.

He dreams that he cannot sleep, because of all the goddamn singing from outside. Because of all the fire and brimstone being preached by Pastor Tom. Who is back to wearing his loincloth, and preaching from atop the scaffold. With a noose around his neck, tied to one of the scaffold's railings. The congregation seems like they've come more to see whether he will hang himself than to hear the good word.

Typical, he thinks, in his dream.

Though he must admit that he, too, is much more curious about how this is all going to end than about the words the man is saying, especially seeing as how he can't make out what the words are, they get lost in the echoes reverberating about the cavernous hall.

Is the other end of the rope really tied to the scaffolding? he wonders, in his dream. *Or is it just a prop?*

He dreams that he thinks that he is dreaming, but is actually awake. He rolls off the bench and crawls his way over to the trailer door. Opens it slightly. Peeks out.

They are singing. They are lifting up their voices to the heavens.

He wants them to see him—to recognize him and call him over to join them—while being simultaneously terrified that they will see him, and recognize him—and know what he has done. That they will know who he has become.

He tells himself, in his dream, that he should not be so afraid. Should not be *sore* afraid. That's how they say it in the Bible. He remembers that much. Remembers asking his father why they said it like that.

Because when you're bad, his father told him, *you get the belt. Then you'll be sore.*

He's remembering these things now—in his dream—because this was the church where his father would take him and his mother when he was a boy. Those people out there, they probably knew his father. Maybe, if they squinted really hard, and searched the cobwebby corners of their fading memories, just maybe they would even recognize him, see the traces of that innocent, six-year-old boy underneath the tattoos and the stubble and the sneer.

Von, why yes! I remember you. Welcoming him into a warm, talcum-scented embrace. *My—look how you've grown.*

My, my—look at the man you've become.

He steps outside. Because he's dreaming, he doesn't notice his foot. Except, because he's dreaming, now he notices it even more. It fucking hurts. Maybe it is broken. Still he hobbles over to the congregation, stops at the rear, stares right down the aisle.

Pastor Tom is preaching, his right hand in the air, holding a book aloft. The morning light slants in from behind him, and gleams blindingly from the gilt lettering on the front cover. He shields his eyes, squints—it is his father's Bible!

He lowers his eyes, sees that Pastor Tom is wearing his Jordans. They look ridiculous paired with a blue-and-white checkered short-sleeve button-down and jeans.

So now we're even, he dream-thinks. *My Bible and my Jordans, for your monkey suit and too-tight penny loafers.*

Somehow, even a preacher got one over on me.

"Join us, brother," Pastor Tom says to him. A few heads turn to stare at him.

Von begins to walk down the aisle. He stops next to an old man wearing enormous glasses and a dark baseball cap with a ship and a bunch of medals on it. The name of the ship is the USS *Vengeance*.

Von asks the man, "Do you know my father?"

When the man shakes his head, confused, he asks the woman sitting beyond him. She looks like Jasmine, beneath her sunhat. Or maybe it's Shelly she reminds him of.

"Do *you* know my father? Do you remember him?"

Pastor Tom is standing next to him. He places his arm around Von's shoulders, guides him back down the aisle.

"The question, my son," Pastor Tom says, "is do *you* know your Father?"

Von can tell, from the way he says it, that the "F" is capitalized. That he's talking about our Lord and Savior. He lowers Von into an empty chair at the rear.

"This is why we are here, on this glorious Sunday morning," Pastor Tom says, as he returns to the front of the congregation. As he walks, he lifts Von's father's Bible high into the air. "We are all here to remember our Father."

Von lists over into the empty chair next to him, prompting the couple sitting in the adjacent chairs to lift up and scoot further down.

All just a dream. Right?

Gotta be.

The singing starts up again. Washes over him, and through him. Lifts him up—on angel's wings—and carries him aloft, into those bright morning sunbeams.

Glory, glory, glory.

He awakes in the trailer. On the bench. Under the rattling AC unit. Facing the door.

It opens, and Pastor Tom climbs the steps. The sunlight beyond him has a different quality. Orange. Warm. Diminished. Smoke drifts up into the light, forming a gauzy haze. The smells and sounds of chicken cooking on the grill, rendered fat sizzling on hot coals, follow Pastor Tom into the trailer.

Pastor Tom stops opposite him, peers down. He now wears a moth-nibbled, paint-stained Florida Gators T-shirt.

"I slept a long time," Von says.

"And yet you are restless," Pastor Tom says, then moves on into the kitchen.

Von has to chuckle. Despite the pain in his wrist, in his foot, coming back to him now, redoubled. Doesn't matter what he says, this crazy coot has some off-the-wall comeback.

Pastor Tom goes back outside carrying paper towels, paper plates, salt and pepper shakers. The door closes with a bang that startles Von fully awake.

He sits up. The package of peas hits the floor with a wet slap. The top of his foot is purple, swollen, sore. He pushes the sole into the floor without standing—it can tolerate at least some pressure. The towel wrapped around his wrist has worked itself loose, and the paper towels beneath have turned crimson and crusty. He'll need to change that, but for now he tightens and reties the towel.

He stands, and sees three strange objects on the table, next to the peas: the mark's car keys and wallet, and the phone Howie gave him. He looks for the preacher's pants and shirt, but there's no sign of them.

Did he take the keys and wallet out of the pockets, and put

them on the table before he passed out? Or did Pastor Tom do that when he found the clothes?

And, if he did it, did he look in the wallet? Did he see this Florida driver's license, in the name of Sanjay T—, with a picture of a man who is definitely not Von?

He steps gingerly down out of the trailer. Still limping, still letting his right take most of his weight. He and Pastor Tom are both barefoot. There are several Tupperware tubs and containers of food on the table: coleslaw, potato salad, Caesar salad, corn on the cob, corn bread. Von lifts the grill lid: two chicken legs, the skin glistens golden brown. They're just about done. He hasn't eaten anything since the burger at Tarzan's.

He's about to ask where all the food came from, but a vague memory of the congregants moving about the yard, rearranging the chairs into smaller groups, sharing food, pops into his head. A potluck. Charity for the dogged old pastor. Did he dream this? Or glimpse it through the trailer door?

He preempts the old man: "The Lord provides."

Pastor Tom nods, scoops some potato salad onto a plate. "Indeed," he says. He lifts his bearded chin toward the parking lot. "I see you have provided yourself with some wheels."

The Mercedes is the only car in the lot, now. It's conspicuous.

"I'm borrowing it."

He needs to move it. Either behind the dumpster, or—better yet—out of here entirely. After dinner.

Pastor Tom opens the grill, squeezes some barbecue sauce over the chicken, spreads it over the skin with the back of a plastic spoon.

Von takes out the phone. It turns on, unlocks, seems to work. He has a signal. He gets onto the internet. Local news, Naples. Crime reports. Shootings.

His story comes up first.

"Tragic Pre-Dawn Shooting in Mandalay Villas" is the headline.

"Ruben A—, 37, was in town with his wife visiting their friends, residents of Mandalay Villas, for the weekend. When he heroically attempted to stop a break-in in progress, the would-be intruder shot him twice, once in the leg, once in the head. First responders rushed him to the hospital, where he is now in critical condition."

So let me get this straight, he thinks. *Darnell invites his buddy Ruben and his wife down for the weekend—knowing that I just got out. Probably thinking if there are other people around, then I won't try anything. But how am I supposed to know that, Darnell? It's not like I'm following your dumb-ass on Instagram or Facebook or some shit.*

And ain't that just like Darnell? Bringing his so-called friends into the mix, to have around as human shields. Willing to sacrifice them, just as he sacrificed me.

It's despicable. I didn't think he would stoop that low. I really didn't.

Really didn't think—

His initial relief changes as he scrolls down, to see an update to the original story announcing that Ruben was pronounced dead at 2:00 that afternoon.

While he was sleeping it off in the trailer.

Of all the luck. You fire six shots, and wouldn't one have to hit this clown in the head? You weren't even aiming high. Aiming for the legs. Just trying to scare the dude. Could barely even hold the gun straight you were in so much pain.

You're a killer now, Von.

Not murder one, though—it wasn't premeditated. He hadn't *wanted* to kill the guy. Hadn't even wanted to kill Darnell.

Shit—with his luck, if it had been Darnell behind the door, all six shots would've missed.

Still, homicide. Manslaughter.

A little further down there is a picture of him, from the shoulders up, looking bored, the orange collar of the FCD jumpsuit visible. "Von Martin, 32."

He is a "person of interest." "Wanted for questioning."

A wanted man.

They catch you for this, and pin it on you—you're going away for the rest of your life. Guaranteed.

Pastor Tom hands him a plate, sagging full of chicken, potato salad, and corn bread.

"Leave it on the table," Von says. "I'll get to it."

But his appetite has vanished. Along with the orange sun, dipping below the tree line.

Time to pay Jasmine a visit—see what the cops got out of her.

CHAPTER
ELEVEN

IT'S close to 11:00 pm by the time he reaches Jasmine's building in Delasol Views. It's a high-rise, one of three towers that overlooks the gulf on one side, a marina on the other. He knows he's taking a chance driving the Mercedes, but Pastor Tom lives down on the south side of town. He can't walk, with his foot—what was he going to do, take the bus, like a chump? He parks the car in the visitors parking lot.

Net take: $427 all told. Not bad... but not great. He's got the guy's credit cards, including an Amex Black, but he knows he can't use those now without giving himself up. Same with the car: worth thousands, but there's no way he can sell it. Not with his blood still darkening the black leather seats.

At the tall glass doors he finds a metal box with a number pad. He enters the number she gave him. Rather than opening the door, it dials up to her apartment. While the phone rings, a name flashes on the little LCD display, "N. Lukacs." Is this the right number? The door clicks and hums; he grabs the handle and pulls. From behind an enormous marble desk, a doorman waves at him; he nods back as he crosses the lobby. A fountain cascades down over a sculpture that looks like somebody tried to make a tower out of a bunch of metal cubes, but when it fell apart just said "fuck it" and welded them together where they'd landed.

She lives on the fourteenth floor, of eighteen. When he presses the button, he realizes that there is no thirteen, the numbers on the panel skip from twelve to fourteen. In other words, she lives on the thirteenth floor, they're just calling it the fourteenth. Pretending.

Like bad luck ain't gonna see right through that.

She's waiting in the open doorway to her apartment as he walks down the hall.

"I wasn't sure you'd really come," she says. She steps back into the apartment.

"My word is my bond, babe."

"What happened to you?" She has seen his bandage. On his way over, he stopped at a drugstore and bought hydrogen peroxide, a butterfly bandage, gauzy wrap, and a wrist brace, then sat in the car and cleaned out the cut, bandaged it, and velcroed the brace over it all. Probably could've used a stitch or two, but he'll survive. "What did you do?"

"I must've twisted it pulling that jabroni out of the car," he says. "No biggie."

"And you're limping?"

"He slammed my foot in the door—didn't you see that? Now *that* shit hurt."

"Poor baby," she says as she closes the door behind him. "Let me take care of you."

He hobbles toward the sliding glass doors to the balcony. "Real swanky place, this."

"I moved here a year ago." She slides open the door, and a humid breeze flutters the curtains in the air-conditioned apartment. "I wanted to live somewhere safe, you know? A building with a doorman, and where I wouldn't have to worry about the hurricanes."

"Bet this is a nice view during the day," he says, looking out over the ocean.

The moon is low, and bright. Reminds him of the moon looking down over him, and Jasmine, and the mark on the beach. *Just last night that was. Is that possible?* So much has happened. Sleeping during the day, being awake at night is screwing with his sense of time.

"I don't know what I was thinking," she says. "It's too expensive. I'm always broke."

She puts her head in her hands, and leans into his side.

He grabs the railing in both hands. Being up this high gives him a strange sense of dizziness, of falling. A sensation that a giant hand might scoop him up and toss him over the edge, down to the pool and the little tiki-hut thatched rooftops dimly lit by orange lamps.

"You never were very good with money," he says, as he turns to reenter the apartment.

"I know."

Another thing he appreciated about Shelly—she never misplaced a dime. Always had her mind on her money.

Maybe a little too much, he realizes, in retrospect.

"Here," he says, once she closes the door. "I got something for you."

"You did?" Her eyes are bright. He winces at the sight of the square bandage at her temple, the hint of a bruise under a caked layer of makeup extending down to her cheekbone.

He pulls his wad from the hip pocket of his shorts. Peels off a bunch of twenties.

"Your cut," he says.

Her shoulders sag. "Oh," she says. "I don't want that."

"You just said you need it." He waves the bills at her.

"I don't pay my rent in cash."

"No, but you can pay for your groceries with cash, and use

the money you don't spend on groceries to pay your rent. Duh."

"Well—duh—I know that, Von. But I don't want money. I thought you were going to say you'd gotten me flowers, or chocolates, or something."

"What good would that shit do you? If you're broke—"

"Flowers would make the apartment look and smell nice. Chocolates would taste good. I haven't had a box of chocolates in a minute."

"So you take the money, and buy some flowers—or whatever you want. How hard is that?"

"But then it's not a gift!"

He shakes his head, and laughs. "I never will understand women. Never happy. Never satisfied. No matter what you do."

"Are you hungry?" she asks. "I picked up some sushi."

"Not a fan," he says.

"I bet you've never even tried it."

"Raw fish? Why would I?"

"Just try it."

She leads him into the kitchen, pulls out a chair for him at a small circular table. A little brushed metal vase holds a single yellow rose, made of fabric. Matching brushed metal salt and pepper shakers and sugar bowl with a little spoon sticking from it flank the vase.

And this is why chicks always be broke, he thinks. *Always buying all this useless shit, and it's always gotta match, or be on trend, or be from some brand.*

She returns to the table with first one large ceramic plate, then another, each covered with an array of brightly colored shapes, reds and oranges and pinks and greens, against the black wrappers and the white rice.

"Looks like cookies," he says. "The fancy kind."

She places one smaller plate in front of him, another at her place. She decants a puddle of brown liquid onto his plate, then onto hers.

"No soy sauce for me," he says. "Too much estrogen."

She goes to the counter, returns with a bottle and sticks it in his face.

"It's no-soy tamari," she says. "I can't do soy with my gluten allergy."

She deposits a dollop of wasabi on the edge of his plate, then on hers. Finally she lays a pair of chopsticks at an angle across his plate, then on hers.

"You're like a geisha," he says.

"What's that?" Her eyes narrow. "Isn't that just Japanese for a prostitute?"

"Nah," he says. "Well, maybe. But they're like really high-class. All they do is serve tea to the guy, but everything has to be done just right. They make a ceremony out of it—you made everything look so perfect, it just reminded me of that."

"Aw," she says, as she pulls out her chair and sits opposite him. "That's nice."

"I don't think they even have sex with the dude. All he wants is to be treated with proper respect."

She is staring at him, chopsticks poised. Waiting for him to make the first move.

He forgoes the chopsticks and picks up a small cylindrical piece in a black wrapper.

"Salmon," she says. "Those are my favorite."

He dunks it in the brown puddle, and pops it into his mouth.

"Weird," he says, barely chewing. "It kinda melts in your mouth."

"And? Do you like it?"

He nods. "Tastes like salty butter."

"See?"

He selects another piece, of a different color and shape.

After a few more, she shows him how to mix the wasabi into the sauce, which adds a whole new dimension.

She gets him to uncork a bottle of white wine. She bought beer for him, but he doesn't want to drink much, so he has some of the wine, which he knows he won't like.

"Don't you want to know about my lovely evening with the cops?" she asks.

"Oh snap!" He pushes back from the table. Somehow he'd forgotten. "How'd it go?"

"Not great," she says, with a shake of her head. "I didn't get home until five. They made me wait until the day shift got in—no sleep—and then they grilled me all morning."

"What did you tell them?"

"Just what you told me to—really, I just described the whole thing."

"They hook you up to a lie detector or anything?"

She shakes her head.

"Did they ask you if you knew me?"

She nods. "I think they saw this"—she waves at the left side of her face—"and thought there's no way they were in on it together. Plus I was crying a lot."

"Good girl."

"I didn't even have to fake it. This shit hurts, Von."

"Had to be done," he says. "Otherwise you'd still be at the station, and they wouldn't believe you for shit."

"I called in sick today, but I can tell Larissa was pissed. I don't know how I'm supposed to go to work tomorrow." Her hand shakes slightly as she lifts the wine glass to her mouth. She takes a long sip.

When she lowers the glass, she looks at him, locks eyes with him. There's a slight tremble there. The hint of a tear forming. She has sacrificed for him. Actions, not words—and hell if her actions haven't shown she's a stand-up chick. He reaches across the small table and covers her hand with his.

"You did good," he says.

"I've been freaking out."

"Real good," he says. "I know it wasn't easy."

"They keep asking the same questions over and over, and I start to think maybe they know something. And then I'm worrying about you on top of it all—"

"I know," he says.

"I can't do this again, Von," she says.

"It's the last time," he says. "I swear—I won't ask you to help me ever again."

"I want to help you." She places her other hand over his, squeezes. "Just not that again."

He extricates his hand, and they resume eating, and drinking in silence, until he asks her how her life has been, these last four years. Since there sure isn't much to tell about his. She makes it sound like she was in just as much of a prison as he was. Wanting a better job, but unable to make the transition.

"We all make our own prisons," he says. Sounds deep. Like something Mr. Counselor Dude would say. Probably *is* something he said.

"It's so true," she says. "I moved here because I wanted to feel safer—but now I feel trapped. Sometimes, when I'm looking at all these bills I can't pay, I feel like I'm in water up to my neck, and drowning. I think I'm having actual panic attacks. My old place was a complete and utter shithole, but I never felt like I couldn't breathe."

They finish, and she stands, takes the little plates to the sink. He rises and brings the serving plates, sets them down on the counter. He refills their glasses with the surprisingly good white wine.

While she's rinsing the dishes and loading them into the dishwasher, she says she can't believe Shelly would divorce him while he was upstate. Can't believe she couldn't wait, not even for the father of her daughter.

"What a bitch," she says, as she stands and closes the dishwasher.

Which is, he knows, what he wants to hear. He nods along —well aware that she's back to running game on him. He can spot game a mile away. *Best believe.*

"Women can't go longer than a month without a man around," he says, with a shrug. "That's just the way it goes."

She pulls off the long yellow rubber gloves, drapes them over the sink divider. Turns to face him, and leans back against the sink.

"Don't suppose you were exactly pining away for me the entire time I was away either."

She smacks him. Across the face.

A complete lack of respect. He can't believe this has just happened.

"I would've been," she says, defiant in the face of his hesitation, "if you'd given me any reason to be!"

He raises his hand—he knows what he has to do. To maintain respect.

She doesn't flinch. But the sight of her already battered face checks him.

Self-control, he reminds himself. *Breathe.*

"Now we're even," he says. "But don't try me again."

They pick up their wine glasses and move to the living room. She sits on the couch, and pats the space next to her, but he sits in an overstuffed armchair. She gets up and sits on his lap, leans into him. Starts kissing him. Her mouth tastes like peppery soy sauce.

He moves his hand up along her thigh, pushes it between her legs, to her inner thigh. She is not wearing any underwear. She hikes up her skirt and opens her legs, slides one knee over his hip and down into the chair's cushions. Presses her breasts into his face.

"Remember how cold you used to be to me?" she whispers into his ear.

"Back then I was cold to every woman who wasn't named Shelly."

Not entirely true, he thinks. *But breasts in the face make it hard to even know what the truth is.*

"Don't even say her name," she says.

"I know." He hikes up her tight skirt, grabs her bare ass in both hands. "I hate the way it sounds, now."

"She never did deserve you." She is breathing heavy now.

"No woman deserves me."

He lifts her leg so he can get out from under her, puts her knee back where it was. She looks over her shoulder at him, and he pushes her forward, so she has to catch herself on the chair back. He pulls down his shorts and kicks out of them. He is hard. He is ready. It's been a long time.

She rears up again, puts one foot on the floor. Turns toward him.

"Let's go to the bedroom," she says.

He shoves her forward. *Think you can slap me?* He drives his knee into the back of her straight leg so she has to bend it and lift it to the chair again, while he grabs her by the hips and pulls her ass back toward him.

"Let's do it nicely," she says.

"Nice ain't how you want it," he says, his voice low and raspy. Doesn't even sound like his own voice—sounds like it's being torn out of his lungs by a demon.

You think you know what it's like to be in prison? For four fucking years?

He drops a gob of spit onto his fingers.

"Von," she says. "Wait—"

"We got all night," he says. "I'm gonna fuck you here—"

"Von, please—"

"—and on the couch—"

"No you won't."

"—in the bed—"

"You're going to get your rocks off…"

"—in the shower—"

"And then you're going to fall asleep. Von—"

"Ain't gonna be nothing nice about it."

"Von, wait. Let's go to the bed. Von—"

"That's right. Say my name."

"Von. Oh, Von. Be nice to me, Von—"

CHAPTER
TWELVE

VON WAKES to the smells and sounds of Jasmine making eggs and bacon and toaster waffles. After breakfast, she spends an hour or two in the bathroom working on her makeup, and in the end manages to camouflage the bruising and hide her swollen eye behind oversized sunglasses and a broad-brimmed sunhat, pulled down low. Around two, she arranges for a grocery delivery, then tells him she needs to get her hair done and run some errands before going to work. She kisses him goodbye, tells him to be good, and leaves him alone in her apartment.

He turns on the large-screen TV to see if there is anything more about the shooting. The news cycle has moved on. At least on cable.

On the internet, he finds a follow-up story.

"This is a horrible tragedy," said a visibly emotional Darnell B—, who was renting the apartment with his girlfriend and her daughter. The victim, Ruben A—, and B— had been best friends since their time in elementary school in Gainesville. "I can't imagine what would motivate a person to do such a thing," B— said. "It's senseless."

Can't imagine, can you, Darnell? Sure about that, buddy?

What I can't imagine is "what would motivate" a person to drag their supposed "best friend" into a beef that you know you started—and that you knew you weren't capable of finishing on your own.

"We can't stay here," B— noted, "it's become too dangerous. I have to think about my girlfriend, and her daughter. They're my priority."

Looks like you finally got your fifteen minutes of fame out of this, didn't you, Darnell? I'm sure you're getting all kinds of sympathy.

Good luck with your move, buddy. Better watch your back the entire way. You won't do anything to avenge your "best friend's" death—but I will. I'll get the real culprit. The one who set him up to take the fall on his behalf.

Good intel, though—they're moving. He has to act soon. How's he ever going to see Tara again if he doesn't know where they are?

Rummaging through the kitchen he finds bottles of tequila and rum and vodka in her pantry—all open and partially consumed, but collecting dust. She's more of a white wine girl. He closes the pantry doors—the last thing he needs is to start day drinking because he's bored. He knows booze will just make him restless.

He's never really been up this high in a building with a balcony before. It's both fascinating and horrifying. The view stretches across the inlet to the mainland beyond. Below and to his left, he can make out the marina—a forest of masts and the occasional flash of white hull as boats move between the slips. As he watches, a sleek fishing boat emerges from the harbor, cutting a white wake as it heads toward open water. Probably some rich asshole heading out for a day of deep-sea fishing, or maybe down to the Keys for the weekend.

Must be nice, he thinks. *Just hop on your boat and disappear whenever you want.*

Another boat follows the first, this one larger, with multiple decks. The *whumpa-thumpa* of the sound system floats up to him all the way up on the thirteenth—or fourteenth—floor. A yacht that costs more than most people make in a lifetime.

Von grips the railing, watching the boats grow smaller as they head toward the gulf. The freedom of it eats at him. All that open water. All those places a man could go if he had the means.

Maybe that's the answer. Maybe that's how I get out of this mess.

He'd never been much of a boat person, but how hard could it be? Point it toward the horizon and go. The Keys, the Bahamas, maybe even further south. Someplace where they'd never think to look for Von Martin.

A third boat catches his attention, bobbing into the marina—smaller, a simple fishing vessel with a single outboard. The kind of boat a regular person might own. The kind a desperate man might be able to... borrow.

From his elevated perch he studies the layout: the security gate, the docks, the fuel pumps. Filing it away for later. Just in case.

A vehicle cruising slowly through the parking lot between him and the marina catches his eye. White SUV, dark green lettering on the side, black bullbars growing out of the bumper, a rack of lights across the roof.

Instinctively, he retreats from the balcony's edge, into the shadows. Below, the SUV drifts among the rows of parked cars, a shark scenting the waters. It comes to a halt almost directly below, in the fire lane. The driver's door opens, and a rotund figure steps down. Lifts a cowboy hat to cover his balding head. Hitches his belt, waddles toward the entrance, disappears from view.

Ah, shit, Von thinks. He slides open the door, and even though he's expecting it, the sharp insistent buzz shattering the apartment's silence causes him to jump.

He creeps to the intercom panel by the front door. The small black-and-white screen shows a grainy image of a man in a cowboy hat with a drooping mustache, aviator sunglasses perched on his fleshy nose.

Alvin.

How did he know about Jasmine? And how did he get her address? Must've paid her a visit. Getting entirely too clever for his own good.

The bell rings again, longer this time. Alvin shifts his weight, leans closer to the camera. Even through the fuzzy feed, Von can see the man's impatience, his certainty that he's onto something.

You want to play games, Alvin? Fine. But I ain't the same man you put away. I play for keeps now. You've got proof of that now.

The sheriff waits another minute. Von stays at the intercom until the bastard turns away. Then he hobbles, still on the balls of his feet—as though Alvin might somehow hear him moving through the apartment all the way down there—to the balcony. Watches that fat fuck amble across the parking lot to his white SUV with green trim.

As he opens the SUV's door, the sheriff tips his head back, angling those aviators toward the upper stories. Von presses himself against the partition separating Jasmine's balcony from her neighbor's. Leans his head around just enough to watch the SUV trundle out of the parking lot, vanish behind a line of palm trees.

He needs to think. Needs to move. Can't just sit here waiting for them to close in.

No—that's just what he wants. Probably only pretending to drive away to lure me out.

Self-control, he reminds himself. *Breathe.*

The reminder is actually necessary: he'd been holding his breath. He unclenches his fists.

Back inside he goes to the kitchen to pour himself a glass of tequila, but then stops himself. Screws the lid back on, puts the bottle back in the pantry, fills the glass with water instead.

Booze only makes it worse. You know this.

He goes back out to the living room and puts the TV on. The Heat are playing, and he watches that until it's over and the Heat have won. Scrolls through YouTube, searches for more news videos about the shooting.

There are two pictures of him they're using. One from right before he went in, in his civvies. He recognizes the picture, and can tell from the way he is slightly stooped forward and reaching down, hands out of the frame, that Tara is clinging to his leg, but they've cropped her out of the image, zoomed in on him from the waist up.

The second one, he's in his orange jumpsuit. This one is cropped closer to his face, but you can still see the orange collar, the white tee underneath. He knows they're not trying to make him look good—knows they want to make him look like a criminal—but still. He looks annoyed in the one with Tara—even though she's not in it—and bored, or maybe high, in the prison pic.

They're still referring to him as a "person of interest."

If you have any information regarding this man's whereabouts, please call the snitch hotline you see on your screen.

Rummaging in her walk-in closet he finds some men's clothes: shorts and Hawaiian floral shirts. Proof she wasn't exactly pining away for him. They're baggy and boomerish but still an upgrade over the tired drip he wore into prison.

Better than an orange jumpsuit.

The sound of Jasmine's keys and bags on the kitchen counter startle him awake. He lifts his cheek from the arm of the sofa. The cable guide is scrolling mindlessly through channels in the thousands. The time says 2:43.

"Hey!" she says, cheerily, as she strides into the room and flops onto the couch next to him. She kicks off her shoes. She smells of sweat, and cigarettes, and booze. She is still wearing her sunglasses. Her densely caked makeup shows cracks and flakes in the harsh light cast by the side table lamp.

"You smell like Tarzan's," he says.

"Thanks a lot," she says.

"I wish I coulda been there," he says. "There's nothing to do up in here."

"No you don't," she says. She heaves a sigh. "That place is such a shitshow. Where'd you get that shirt?"

She picks at the hem of his sleeve, which hangs down to his elbow.

"Your closet," he says.

"Oh." She frowns, lifts her sunglasses, perches them on top of her head. "I guess I do recognize that."

"Thought you never had men over," he says, with a smirk.

"He was special," she says. She reaches for the remote. "For a minute. I got some food for us."

She switches over to YouTube. The results of his recent searches are still up on the screen.

With the other remote, he switches the television power off. Too late, she is already frowning.

"What was that?" she asks.

"I'm starving," he says. He holds his hand out, to help her up off the couch. "Let's eat. What'd you get?"

"Chinese," she says.

"It's like you can read my mind," he says.

He enters the kitchen, wades into a thick scent of hot and spicy grease, starts pulling styrofoam food containers out of plastic bags. One of them has written on it in black sharpie, "Nora."

N. Lukacs. Nora.

He remembers a night at Tarzan's where she'd told him her real name. Her shift was over, and they were having a drink together. Playing footsie under the table.

"Cops bugging you today at all?" he asks, as she sets the table.

He watches her closely, but his question doesn't seem to bother her. Maybe Alvin knew about her from before. Maybe he was just following his own hunch.

"At work?"

He shrugs. "Anywhere."

She shakes her head.

"Your friend come to see you?"

"Sanj?" She gives a short, sharp bark of a laugh. "I don't think he'll ever be back."

"You never know." He grabs her ass. "Once they get a taste of Jasmine…"

She bats his hand away, but she's hiding a smile. He scoops rice onto the plates, and tops it with kung pao chicken and five-pepper beef. He fills her wine glass, pours himself a glass as well. He pulls out her chair, and she sits in it, and he pushes her in under the table. The kitchen is full of warmth and good smells. Good vibes.

She raises her glass, and he lifts his.

"What are we toasting?" she asks.

Crap. She wants him to say something sweet, or something deep.

"To new beginnings," he says. He clinks his glass against hers.

"I like that," she says. "To new beginnings."

They eat, and she tells him about the latest drama among Larissa and the dancers, and the bouncers, and Howie refusing to exercise any control over the situation.

Howie, he thinks. *Maybe he gave up Jasmine's address.*

"You guys should have a show," he says. "Real Strippers of Tarzan's."

"Oh my God!" She smacks his arm. "We say that all the goddamn time. It's a fucking soap opera."

She sure got a mouth on her, ain't she?

"People would watch it," he says.

"I know, right?"

She serves him seconds. Between the wine, and the food, and having a laugh with Jasmine, he's feeling pretty good.

"You're so good to me," he says. "Better than I deserve."

She washes down a mouthful with a swig of wine.

"This could've been us all these years," she says.

He shakes his head. Drops his fork on his plate.

"Women," he says. "They never let you forget your past sins, do they?"

"You know how many late nights I stayed at the club listening to you go on and on about how great this Shelly woman was?" she asks. "Where is she now?"

"Gainesville, maybe? Don't know, don't care."

"I was there for you that whole time, Von. I never would've cut out on you. Never would've done you dirty like that."

"Yeah, you say that now." He pushes back from the table. "But once you had me, it wouldn't have lasted."

She looks up at him. Seeks out his eyes with hers. Bright puppy dog eyes. He knows it's a put-on. He knows it's an act. It's not that it's convincing so much as it shows him that she wants to be on his good side.

She stands up, comes around behind him, starts rubbing his shoulders.

"Let's not fight," she says.

"I'm just jumpy," he says. "Tense."

"We need to take you down a notch," she says.

After they take each other down a notch—maybe even two—she hops up out of bed to visit the bathroom. After rummaging around in her closet for a minute or two, she returns with a leather pouch.

"We getting kinky?"

"No, silly," she says. She shakes out a deck of oversized cards, removes a rubber band from around them. "Let's do a reading."

"What do you mean? Read what?"

She spreads colorful cards out on the bed between them, unlike any deck of playing cards he's ever seen. "These are my tarot cards."

"Like, fortune-teller cards?"

She smiles. An eager little girl.

And while that is endearing and all, he is not trying to see what his future holds.

"I don't think that's a good idea," he says.

"Why not?" She pouts.

"You know you live on the thirteenth floor, right? That's some bad luck right off the bat."

"It's the fourteenth."

"But there is no thirteenth. Which means—"

"I know what it means," she says. "But they call it the fourteenth. So I consider it the fourteenth."

"In other words, you tell yourself what you want to hear," he says. "That's all these cards will do, too. Tell us what we want to hear."

"No," she says. She starts scooping the cards together. Stuffing them into the leather pouch. "I just wanted to—"

"Are you crying?"

"Why are you so mean?" Her shoulders slump, and she folds her face into her hands.

He sits up in the bed, naked, careful of his bruised left foot. He picks up the cards from in between them—his right wrist still wrapped in the drugstore brace—and sets them on the nightstand. Grabs her hands, holds them in his.

"Listen," he says.

He leans toward her. Places his mouth on her warm neck.

"Sh-sh-sh. Come on, now."

She smells of sweat and makeup and shampoo and cigarettes and perfume and Chinese food and sex. She smells of woman. And now tears, too.

"It's just—" he begins. Hesitates. "This has been a real nice night. You know? What if the cards tell us something bad? Why end the night on a sour note?"

He feels her nodding against him, her forehead digging into his shoulder, her hair catching in his stubble.

"We got a good thing going here." He wraps his arms around her. "Why let some mystical mumbo-jumbo ruin it all? Tell us that it can't possibly last? You know?"

She sniffles loudly in his ear.

"You're right," she says. She pulls back from him, blinking back tears, swiping at her cheeks with her fingers, long nails painted bright red. "I guess I'm just freaking out. This is all happening so fast."

"We're both on edge," he says. He leans back into the bed. "We should get some sleep."

She reaches for the light, switches it off, joins him. Stretches herself out on top of him, throwing one leg over his hip, one arm over his shoulder, nuzzles her face into his chest and neck. And even though her weight is making him hot, and preventing him from rolling over onto his side so he can sleep, he stays there, her human pillow, holding her. Stroking her back with his fingernails. Until her breathing starts to come heavy and regular.

He hardly needs magic cards to tell him this can't last.

But why put a curse on it?

Why summon that end before its appointed time?

CHAPTER
THIRTEEN

HIDING OUT.

He doesn't like it.

He's a man of action. The forced inactivity is driving him crazy.

Might as well be back in prison. Can't go outside, except for the balcony.

He needs to move the car. If Alvin or some other clown comes back and makes a systematic sweep of the area, they'll find it. But he should wait till the sun goes down. Too many security cameras around.

Out on the balcony, he closes his eyes and feels the hot Florida sun on his eyelids, his cheeks. His hands grip the warm metal railing atop the low concrete wall.

He opens his eyes and peers over the edge again. Down at the pool, the tiki huts. A handful of people stretched out on lounge chairs, or heads bobbing in the pale blue water.

Can't even go for a swim. Can't do anything.

Thirteen floors. What would that drop be like?

If you had to pick a way to go out, would this be it? Would it feel like flying?

Nah—you'd spend the whole way down regretting it, looking back up at the balcony and wishing for those last few seconds that you were up there again and able to rethink it, and make a different decision. You wouldn't be able to enjoy it, at all.

Horrible way to go.

He retreats to the air conditioning. He channel-surfs. He snacks. Each time he opens the pantry he considers the bottles of booze there. Each time he resists, proud of himself for doing so.

But he knows it can't last.

So he's out the door. Time to move the car. Time to move, period.

The Mercedes takes him first through wealthy neighborhoods, that seem untouched by the storms. As he steers away from the sea, he comes across more empty lots, more piles of rubble raked together awaiting collection, a few ruined strip malls still boarded up and vacant. Everywhere new buildings are going up on massive stilts of concrete and rebar. Four years changes a place. Just like they change a person.

Gaynor Elementary sits squat and beige. Portable classrooms flank the main building, lined up like dominoes, connected by flimsy-looking aluminum sunshades. The clock on the dash says 2:33. If Shelly has her in public school—and he's not sure how she would afford anything else—then this is the one she'd go to.

He parks across the street where he can see the front entrance and the bus loading zone. Not directly in front. Not where he's going to be conspicuous. A maintenance worker pushes a cart across the parking lot.

He used to do all right in school, back when he was a kid. Wasn't always a fuckup.

He remembers his father dragging him over to talk to Pastor Tom after church one day. Telling the pastor about how his head was always in the clouds. About how he needed some discipline.

"He looks like a smart kid," Pastor Tom had said, squatting down to Von's level. "I see him reading all the time."

"I wish he wouldn't," his father said, frowning down at him. "But at least that way he keeps still."

Pastor Tom had reached for the book he was holding—what was it? Probably that series about a mouse warrior—Redwall? Matthias the mouse, in Mossflower Woods? He read the shit out of those.

"This looks way more interesting than my sermons," Pastor Tom said, with a gentle laugh.

"They're boring," Von said. He felt bad as soon as the words were out of his mouth—and then his father's hand clamped down on his shoulder.

"Say you're sorry."

"It's okay," Pastor Tom said.

"I don't understand them," Von said. "I get lost."

"You don't even try," his father said.

"I did try."

"Once."

"Keep reading," Pastor Tom said, handing the book back to Von. He stood up, to address his father. "He'll come to the right book when it's his time to do so."

Now that he thinks about it, that was probably around the time when his father showed him the page in the Bible where his name would go. *Should* go. If he earned it.

Ain't happening now, is it?
Nah. Not likely.

The school bell rings, sharp and piercing. Within seconds, kids start streaming out. Bus riders form ragged lines by numbered signs.

Von scans the crowd, but there are so many of them, all

moving and shouting and pushing. How is he supposed to pick out one six-year-old girl in all this chaos?

Then he sees her.

She's in line for Bus #7, wearing a pink backpack almost as big as she is. Her hair is pulled back in a ponytail, and she's talking animatedly to another girl beside her. She looks... happy. Normal. Like any other kid whose biggest worry is whether she has enough lunch money or remembered her homework.

My daughter, he thinks. The words feel strange in his head. *Tara.*

She's grown so much. She seems taller than when he saw her at Shelly's, now that she's not hiding away from him, burying herself in her mother's embrace. She stands with her feet planted, gestures with her hands as she's talking. None of the timid clinging he remembers from that disastrous meeting.

Maybe if it was just me and her, he thinks. *Maybe without Shelly here to poison her against me, maybe then she wouldn't be so scared.*

What if he approached her now? Just walked over casually, said hello? Would she even recognize him?

He knows it's a bad idea. Too many witnesses, too many adults around. What if she screamed? What if she ran? What if she pointed her finger at him and said—

A tap on his passenger window makes him jump in his seat. He removes his hand from the door handle where it had been tensing, ready to pull. A middle-aged woman in a school polo shirt gestures for him to roll down the window.

"Sir? Are you picking up a student?"

"What?"

"If you're here for pickup, you need to get in line with the other parents." She points to a queue of cars snaking around the building. "You can't just park and wait here."

"I was just—"

She's frowning now. She doesn't recognize him.

"School policy. For safety."

Von glances back at the bus lines. Tara is moving toward Bus #7. Her pink backpack disappears behind the yellow exterior.

"Sorry," he tells the woman. "My bad."

He presses the ignition—pressing a button rather than turning a key still feels strange—when a white sheriff's SUV drifts slowly past the school. Tinted windows prevent him from seeing who is behind the wheel, or in which direction the driver's eyes are scanning.

Time to go.

He pulls out carefully, forcing himself not to speed. In the rearview, Bus #7 coughs to life and lumbers toward the street, his daughter somewhere inside.

At least I saw her, he thinks. *At least I know she's okay.*

He drives back toward Jasmine's, looking for a place to ditch the car, far enough away where it won't be found, but not so far that walking will make his still-throbbing foot worse. His breathing is shallow. His hands are shaking.

He leaves the car on a side street not far away. If the cops find it, well, it was good while it lasted. They'll find some of his blood—he cleaned it as best he could, but he knows they'll be way more thorough than he ever could be.

Besides, he knows he's not just a "person of interest."

He knows they don't just want to ask him some questions.

He has calmed down. Part of him feels relieved. Grateful, even. *At least the shooting doesn't seem to have touched her. That's the last thing I'd want.*

But another part of him feels more isolated than ever. Knowing that the last thing she needs is him back in her life.

Bringing all this noise and destruction. All this chaos.

Back at the apartment, he searches through the couple of shelves Jasmine has crammed full of paperbacks, looking for something to read. All that time in the joint, and he didn't read a single book. But maybe he can pick it up again now. It's not too late. Keep his nose clean.

But they're all romance novels. The books on the top shelf have dark spines like horror novels—but they're just romance novels about vampires and werewolves. She really is a hopeless romantic.

He's sprawled on the couch watching television when Raul's smug face appears on the screen, in an ad for RTG Construction. "Where we build your dreams," he promises.

Wow, Von thinks. *Ads on cable. You know those ain't cheap. Homeboy really has hit it big.*

What was it he said? Making more money legally than illegally. Seems like that's everybody, these days.

Everybody but me.

He went to work for Raul the summer he was supposed to be finishing high school and getting his diploma. That fall his mother started getting sick. Raul stood by him, he'll give him that. Even chipped in some money.

He brought Von into his office, had him sit down on the other side of the desk. Von thought he was in trouble for something—this was before he had stolen a single thing. Before he found his calling.

But no, he was writing Von a check. For a thousand dollars. He couldn't believe it. He'd never seen someone just give another person an amount like that, no strings attached.

There's always strings, though, ain't there.

As he handed it to him, Raul had said—and this really hit home—"Beg, borrow, or steal, a man's gotta do whatever a man's gotta do to live up to his responsibilities, to do right by his family. By his *people*."

That was the bolt from the blue.

It was like he was even telling me: kid, go get yours. Fuck these rich people in their fancy houses.

Wasn't long after that when he started stealing. With principles, though: always after work hours, never from clients—just from their neighbors.

Whoever says there is no honor among thieves don't know Von.

Then, maybe a year, year and a half later, his mother dies, too. That's when he kicks it into overdrive. Also when he starts getting a little sloppy, what with the drinking, and the drugs. Flashing the cash when they're out at the club. Noticing Raul giving him the side-eye—but he's grieving, you know? He's going through it. Drowning his sorrows, as they say.

Raul's not asking any questions, so long as Von is treating him to bottle service, getting him lap dances, breaking off a hundo here and there.

And all this time Raul is always on about how the game is rigged against us little guys, how you gotta chisel away if you want to make a profit. What's his favorite line? If you aren't cheating you're falling behind.

But when he starts to suspect what Von's really up to—because it's starting to bleed into work hours as well—all those so-called "principles" go out the window.

"Where we build your dreams."

Building his own goddamn dream, about his own dumb-ass self. Who got busted first, Raul? Who covered for you when you were in your minimum-security country club?

The more he thinks about it—and he's got nothing but time to think—the more he starts to realize who it probably was that ratted him out.

Sun sets. Night falls. Von reheats leftover soggy scraps of Chinese food.

When Jasmine comes in, much later, the crash of her keys on the counter tells him something is off.

In the kitchen, she's crying, head in hands. He wonders if she knows about the shooting.

But no. The cops had come by again, asking more questions, about the carjacking. And between them showing up, and her sicking out the night before, Larissa's been threatening to fire her. She's sure she's going to get canned.

"They're not tryna fire you," Von says.

"What do you know about it?" Her face is red, her mascara streaked.

She goes to the pantry, pulls out the bottle of tequila. Pours herself a glass. He sets a second glass down on the counter. Might as well join her.

"Howie won't let her fire you," he says, as he follows her and the bottle of tequila into the living room. She sits on the couch, and he sits next to her. "He knows me and you are tight."

"That might not be the good thing you think it is."

"Were they asking about me?"

"About you. About that night. About whether I've seen you since." She pulls her legs up, wraps her arms around her knees. "I told them no, obviously."

"You are one stand-up babe." He places his hand on the back of her neck, massages the tense muscles there. The makeup trying to hide her bruises has flaked and cracked and been partially swiped away.

I put the mark on her, he thinks. *The mark of vulnerability.*

"I saw Tara today," he says.

"What?" She blinks back tears and turns toward him. "You went out?"

"I was going crazy in here."

"Where did you see her? Was Shelly there?"

He shakes his head. "At her school. Watched her get on the bus, that's all. Just had to see if she's okay, you know?"

"Von, that's—" She seems to think better of whatever she was going to say. "Are you okay?"

"Of course."

She reaches for the remote, lifts it toward the TV, but then doesn't press the button.

"I've been thinking about what you said." She lowers her hand. "About getting out of this shithole."

"And?"

"Where would we go? I mean, like, really? What would we do?"

He takes a last swallow, sets his glass down on the coffee table. In the dim light, her bruises have faded to yellow shadows.

"South," he says. "Like I told you. The Keys, the Caribbean. Somewhere they'll never think to look."

"What are we going to do—steal a boat?"

"We'll borrow one. Rich folks have insurance."

She laughs, a short, sharp, humorless bark. "You make it sound so easy."

"It is easy. The hard part is deciding. Committing."

She's quiet again, staring at the silent TV screen.

"What about my apartment?" She says this softly, as though asking herself the question. "What about my things? My life here."

"What life?" The words sound harsher than he intended, but he pushes on. "You're broke, you hate your job, you're living on the thirteenth floor pretending it's the fourteenth. What is it you would miss?"

She flinches like he's slapped her.

"I'm not trying to be mean," he says, softening his voice.

"I'm just saying—you can't steal second while standing on first."

That's a Mr. Counselor Dude special, right there.

"And you think running away with you might work?"

"I can't stay here," he says.

She nods slowly, like she's trying to convince herself of something.

"We just need another day or two," he says. "For this heat to cool down."

"It's March," she says. "It's only going to get hotter."

"I mean the cops," he says. But she's right about both.

"We don't have to decide now," he says. He stands, moves behind the sofa, starts kneading her shoulders with both hands. "Let's get you out of these clothes, and into the shower."

"I don't think—" she starts to say.

"I'm gonna give you a massage," he says.

"Really?"

"I've put you through hell. It's the least I can do."

After she emerges from the shower, he pats the bed. "You want lotion? Or baby oil?"

"Lotion, please."

She drops the towel and lies face down on the floral bedspread.

He kneels on the bed next to her, and starts working the lotion into her shoulders, her back, her buttocks.

"That feels so nice," she says. "You're being really nice to me."

"I put the mark on you," he says. "Those bruises, they just make you more of a target. Once people see you've been beaten on, they think that gives them the license to do more of the same."

She sighs. Her shoulders are relaxing into the massage.

"That's why Larissa's being such a bitch about things."

He alternates kneading with stroking, caressing. The skin on her back is rough, and full of moles, tanned leather left out to dry. But the lotion is making it pliable again.

"You gotta be careful," he says. "Because some people know what to look for, you know? Sharks."

"You think I don't know this already?"

"All right." He walks on his knees to the edge of the bed. He stands up. His lower back was starting to cramp up from leaning over her anyway. His right wrist, even with the brace, is aching from working his fingers into her.

"I'll just shut up and not say anything," he says.

She rolls over, onto her side. He hates to admit it, but she is looking pretty busted up.

"It's been a really bad night," she says. "I don't want us to be fighting, too."

"Maybe don't be such a bitch to me, then."

"I'm not," she says. She pulls the bedcover back. "Not now."

He switches off the light. In the dark, we're all just mouths, and skin, and body parts. And the lavender perfume of lotion.

CHAPTER
FOURTEEN

THE NEXT DAY Von spends watching animal documentaries. He doesn't have any patience for people anymore. Animals are so much more pure. Hunt or be hunted. Kill or be killed. They're all out there trying to get over on each other, but they all understand this about each other. They've all adapted to their roles.

They're all survivors. Nobody's an engineer, or a businessman, or a plumber.

They're all thieves. All out to take as much as they can get, while still getting away with it.

A cheetah is crouching and twitching, about to spring after a gazelle, when the doorbell rings. Not the angry buzzer from downstairs—this is an artificially cheery *ding-dong* right at the apartment door. Someone is directly outside.

Von mutes David Attenborough's soothing voice—fortunately he didn't have the volume up very high, and the dramatic pursuit music hadn't kicked in yet.

Alvin. Has to be. Back with a warrant this time.

The bell rings again, followed by three firm knocks.

Von pads barefoot to the bedroom. His gun is in the

nightstand drawer, the weight of it familiar in his palm. He checks the cylinder—six fresh rounds.

Another knock, more insistent now.

Von moves back toward the kitchen, gun down along his thigh. He positions himself near the breakfast nook where he can see the front door but stay out of the sightline of the peephole.

"Ms. Lukacs?" A man's voice, muffled but clear through the door. "Ms. Lukacs, this is David Chen from Delasol Property Management."

Not Alvin—but he might be standing next to this guy.

"Ms. Lukacs, we need to discuss the status of your lease agreement. Your account is currently four months and two weeks in arrears, totaling ten thousand seven hundred and thirty-six dollars, including late fees and penalties."

Von reminds himself to breathe. Relaxes his grip on the gun, relieved that this has nothing to do with him.

Three months behind? No wonder she's considering—

"Per the terms of your lease agreement, we are required to provide formal notice that legal proceedings will commence if payment is not received within seventy-two hours. This includes potential eviction proceedings and collection actions that may impact your credit rating."

More knocking.

"Ms. Lukacs, please open the door so we can discuss payment arrangements and avoid formal legal action."

Part of him wants to open the door, show this bureaucratic dipshit what real problems look like. Instead, he lets the man talk to an empty apartment.

"I'm going to slide some paperwork under your door. Please review it carefully. We really don't want to pursue eviction, Ms. Lukacs, but our hands are tied if we don't see some good faith effort to address this situation."

A manila envelope slides under the door, thick with legal documents.

"You have my card. Call me by Thursday. After that, everything goes to our legal department and it will be out of my hands."

Von has started to think that David Chen has left, when his voice filters meekly through the door, barely audible: "I won't be able to help you anymore."

Hm—I wonder how he was helping her, exactly.

Footsteps retreat down the hallway. He waits until he hears the elevator ding before moving to the front door. He peers through the peephole—empty hallway.

He picks up the envelope. It's not sealed, the flap held in place by folding metal arms. Legal jargon, payment schedules, notices of default. All very official; all very final.

Doesn't that explain some things? Girl's about to get thrown out on her ass, sees me as her white knight.

The irony isn't lost on him. Here he is, a wanted man hiding in the apartment of a woman who's about to lose that same apartment. Two people with nowhere to go, clinging to each other like drowning swimmers. Dragging each other down.

He leaves the envelope on the kitchen counter. She'll see it when she gets home. She already knows the situation better than anyone.

The animal documentaries have lost their appeal. All those predators and prey, hunters and hunted. Not much room for comedy in the animal kingdom.

He finds himself on the balcony, staring at the marina again, watching the boats come and go, the distance and height making them look like tiny toys. Rich people's toys, just out of reach.

The heat and the sun drive him back into the AC. He tries to read one of her vampire romances, promising spine-tingling chills and scorching passion in equal measure, but it takes way too long to get going on either account. Next thing he knows, he's missed the sunset.

He's already eaten all the leftovers in Jasmine's kitchen. Her gluten allergy means there's no bread in the house, or cereal, or pasta, or crackers, or pretzels, or any of the sort of food he would usually snack on. He's past the point of eating because he's bored—he's genuinely hungry. And it's only ten o'clock. He's got a long way to wait until she comes back from work with dinner.

He's considering going out to try to rustle up something —maybe risk a drive-thru—when the sound of keys in the door surprise him.

He ducks into the living room, just in case it isn't her. He could never live in a high-rise apartment like this: there's no back door, no easy escape.

Except for the balcony. The one-way ticket.

But the thud and rattle of her leather backpack and car keys on the kitchen counter tell him it's her.

When he enters the kitchen, she straightens and wipes her hands across her cheeks.

Her mascara is streaked, making her look deranged. She's been crying.

His heart sinks. *She knows.*

"How could you?" she asks.

"How could I what?"

Never volunteer any information until you know how much the other person knows.

"You went to see Shelly."

"No I didn't."

"I saw it on the news, Von!"

"I went to see Tara. When I first got out. But that was days ago."

"So why do the cops say you shot a guy at their house?"

"That's not what they're saying. Did you even read the article? No charges have been filed. There's no warrant out for my arrest. I'm just a person of interest."

"So you know about this?"

"Of course I know about it. They want me for questioning."

"Why don't you go answer their questions?"

"Because who do you think they're going to pin it on? The con with no money and no lawyer. Don't be stupid."

"So that's why you're here," she says. "You're hiding out. If it wasn't for the cops looking for you, you would never have even come here."

"That's not true," he says. He steps toward her, but she raises her hands, not in "I surrender" mode, but in "Don't touch me" mode. He backs away, raises his own hands.

"Maybe at first," he says. *Concede some truth—to seed the lie.* "But you've been really good to me, Jasmine. I really like it here."

He steps toward her again.

"I really like you."

"You're so full of shit, Von," she says. "I knew I shouldn't have trusted you."

"You really think I'm just going to roll over to Shelly's place at four in the morning and shoot some guy I don't even know?"

"I don't know what to think," she says. "I don't have any idea what you're doing when I'm not there."

"How did you hear about it?" he asks. "Were there cops at Tarzan's?"

"Larissa said something about how she always googles any man before she starts hooking up with him. To see if they've been in prison or anything like that."

Now his shoulders slump. "But you already knew I was in prison!"

"I wanted to see if anything else turned up."

"And you got what you wanted. I hope you're happy."

"How are you going to get custody of Tara now?" she asks. "How are you even going to see her?"

"I'm telling you," he says, "I had nothing to do with it! I'm innocent!"

"Well, they're not going to believe you." She opens the fridge, pulls out a nearly empty bottle of white wine. "*I* don't believe you."

He sits at the table, while she pours the wine into a glass. She leans against the counter, takes a sip of the wine. Contemplates the refrigerator.

Turns toward him.

"What now?" she asks.

"I guess it's time for me to go," he says.

"You don't have anything else to say for yourself?"

"You've made up your mind," he says, with a shrug. "You've decided I'm guilty. I've seen how this goes. At this point, nothing I do or say is going to change your mind."

He goes into the bedroom to retrieve his old clothes, washed and folded in a plastic Publix bag. And his gun. The grand sum of his worldly possessions.

She follows after him, wine threatening to slosh over the rim.

"What am I supposed to think, Von?"

"I haven't even been *charged* with anything," he says, louder now. He lowers his tone. "But the facts don't matter to you. You have a *feeling*—and you know what? You should trust that feeling. You go, girl. Keep right on stepping."

He moves toward the door. She lays her hand on his elbow.

"Von," she says. "Wait—"

He stops and turns toward her. "I heard a lot of talk about 'oh, I would have waited for you,' and 'oh, I would never do you dirty like Shelly'—but that's all it was. A lot of talk."

"But this is different—"

"Doesn't seem any different to me," he says. "Just a typical chick, abandoning ship when we hit some chop."

He raises his finger, points it at her nose. "Don't think—*not for one second*—that you're any different."

He shrugs off her hand, continues toward the door. Reaches for the handle.

"For a minute there, you had me believing you might be different," he says. "That's on me."

She places her hand over his. Leans her back into the door.

"You said we were going to run away together," she says. "Once you got custody sorted."

"Custody is the least of my concerns," he says.

"What about us?" she says. "What about me? Am I even a concern?"

"Are you an anchor?" he asks, hand still on the door handle, though her ass is pressing into his thumb, and his wrist. "Or a sail?"

"What does that even mean?"

He leans closer to her. Looks down on her. Without bringing himself to touch her.

"Are you helping me? Or holding me back?" he asks. "Are you part of the solution? Or part of the problem? You gotta decide right now. 'Cause if you ain't on Team Von, I gotta jet."

"I don't want to be an accomplice," she says. "I don't want to get in trouble."

"First of all, I haven't been charged with anything," he says. "Second, if you don't know about it, you can't be charged, either. So that's on you, for googling me. That was dumb."

"So this is somehow my fault?"

"They don't say 'ignorance is bliss' for nothing."

She is leaning toward him, but at the same time doesn't seem willing to remove her weight from the door so he can pull it open.

"How are we going to get out of this, Von?"

"We just gotta let this heat blow over," he says. "A few more days, and we're out of here. I promise."

"Oh, Von," she says. "It all seems so goddamn... *hopeless*."

He presses into her, presses her up against the door. He lifts his hand from the door handle, drops it to her thigh.

"Thought you said you were a hopeless romantic," he whispers.

Later, he leaves the bed, leaves Jasmine faintly snoring. He crosses through the living room, steps naked out onto the balcony. The night air is warm against his skin. It's like stepping into a shower of moonlight. In the pre-dawn stillness, he can even hear the surf washing in, receding. Washing in, receding. He matches his breathing to the waves.

If he were a smoker, this would be the perfect moment for a cigarette. Just a little something to occupy his hands while he contemplates. Instead he grips the railing, and does some leaning pushups in time with the waves until a bit of sweat beads his forehead, his lower back. Keeping his breathing in time as well.

It's all down to Raul, isn't it?

This is all happening because Raul couldn't just say yes, *come work for me.*

I got you, bro. Four little words.

He had the opportunity, in that moment, to step up, and take responsibility for "his people"—just like he lectured you about, back when mom was sick.

Hypocrite.

That's all he had to do—no skin off his back—and that would've changed the entire course of events. Would have avoided this whole pathetic tragedy.

Think about it: I would've been like, okay, now I got a job, I got some money coming in, let me find a motel to spend the next couple of nights until I get that first paycheck, and then we'll see about finding something more permanent. Get that paycheck, that permanent address, and now we can take that to the bank and open an account, and take it all to the court and say, hey, I got a place, I got some money. All I want is to see my daughter.

That ain't asking for much.

We got off on the wrong foot, me and Tara. That threw me, I have to admit. Didn't see that one coming. Didn't steel my heart—didn't think I needed to.

So maybe I went into that meeting with Raul with a negative mindset.

Nah—don't get it twisted: he was big-leaguing you right off the bat, making you wait in his office. If you hadn't shown up at the gate he never would've seen you. He would've always been in some meeting, or out at some job site. Trying to pretend like his past ain't his.

Like he's somebody different now, just because he has some coin.

I don't care how much money I have, don't care how big I score—hell, I could win the lottery, and I'll never fucking change. I'll always stay true to who I am.

All he had to do was show me a little respect.

And we wouldn't be in this boat right now.

He touches his middle finger to his thumb, and flicks an imaginary butt over the side. Watches the glowing red ember drop down past the balconies beneath and disappear into the darkness.

CHAPTER
FIFTEEN

"C'MON MAN, what're you doing? Bugging my customers, telling them to come out and meet some guy in the parking lot by the dumpsters? Really, dude?"

Howie shifts his considerable bulk from side to side.

Probably more annoyed about having to get his fat ass out of his chair and waddle out into the humidity than anything else.

"I knew I shouldn't go inside," Von says, "because of the cameras."

"There are cameras everywhere!" Howie says. "You think there aren't cameras out here? This looks like we're doing a drug deal back here."

"It's dark!"

"The cops keep coming around, man." Howie is waving his hands. "They're looking for you. They know this is a place you frequent. They know you were here before!"

"What did you tell them?"

Howie drops his hands, stops his frantic dancing.

"Howard?"

"I told them you stopped by," he admits. "I'm not gonna

lie to the cops, dude. I got a business to think about. I got a family."

"No shit?" *News to me—unless he told me this already?* He extends his hand, which Howie reluctantly shakes. "Congratulations, Howie. You marry one of your dancers?"

"What? No way. Remember Joan, from high school?"

"Joan of Arkansas!"

Howie nods, with a slight grimace at the old nickname. "Kids?"

"Two. A boy and a girl."

"My man." Von releases Howie's hand, and he snatches it back. "You been busy."

"It's been kinda crazy around here," he says.

"I won't hold you up, Howard. I feel like I gotta call you Howard now. Look at you—all grown up."

Howie hangs his head and smiles. "Yeah," he says.

"I'm proud of you," Von says. "You've come along way since sophomore year, when I took you under my wing."

"That was a long time ago, Von," he says. "Ancient history."

"But still history. Still the way things happened."

"Yeah. Listen, I should get back inside. You want me to send out some food or something?"

"No," Von says, though the thought of another burger does make his stomach do a little somersault. "I just wanted to know if you heard anything about Shelly and Darnell. About their whereabouts."

"You sure you want to be fucking with them, right now?" Howie asks. "They must have a restraining order on you. Maybe even round-the-clock protection."

"I just need an address," Von says. "For court filings."

"I haven't heard anything," Howie says. "I haven't seen Darnell since you got busted."

"I'm not even mad about Shelly," Von says. "But he's

trying to steal my daughter, man. You're a father now—you know how that would eat away at your guts, right?"

Howie nods, but insists, "If I knew anything, I'd tell you."

"How about Fedge—you seen him lately?"

Howie shakes his head. "Haven't seen him in ages."

"Max? Max-a-million?"

Howie turns slightly toward the rear door, then back to Von. Just a little hitch. Barely even noticeable.

"He's still around. Stops in once in a while."

"How about tonight?"

"Haven't seen him."

"You sure about that? Howard?"

"I don't screen every customer that walks in the door, Von. I got more important shit to be doing."

"Like getting one of your dancers to blow you, amirite?"

Howie hangs his head sheepishly again. "You know it's not like that, Von. It's a business."

"Just giving you a hard time," Von says. "Relax."

"I gotta get back inside," Howie says. "You sure I can't send something out?"

"I'm good," Von says. *Too proud*, he thinks. *Your pride doesn't always serve you.* "Just wanted a little info."

And you've given me all I need.

He reaches out his hand, and when Howie timidly puts his into Von's, he pulls Howie into him and gives him a bear hug, reaches up to pound him firmly on the back.

"Congratulations," he says, voice muffled by Howie's shoulder. They separate. "So proud of you, kid. You done good."

"Take care of yourself, Von."

"I always do."

He knows Howie. He's played cards with Howie. He's put Howie on the spot before. He knows Howie's tells.

And that little hitch of his has given me a hunch.

Max is in there. Right now.
I can feel it.

He walks up the block, crosses the street, then down a couple of blocks. Settles on the bus stop across the street from the entrance to Tarzan's. It's a little conspicuous, maybe, directly under a street light, but nobody coming out of Tarzan's is going to deign to notice a poor schlub waiting for the bus. It doesn't give him a view of the back door, but customers aren't supposed to use that anyway.

Perhaps most importantly, he'll be able to sit while he waits. Give his foot a rest. Still an hour before last call. Maybe two. He shifts the .38 from tucked into his belt, to the deep front pocket of his shorts. As he does, he unloads it, shoves the fistful of bullets into his other pocket. Doesn't want his bad luck fucking up his plans even further.

He and Darnell and Fedge and Max all used to work on the same crew, and come here every Friday. *Just got paid, time to get laid.* That was the mantra, anyway. Sometimes it even worked out like that.

A bus pulls up to the stop, and the door opens for him. Von waves it away dismissively.

"I'm the last one you'll see tonight," the driver says. She is a squat black woman, who looks like she has fused into the elevated chair and steering wheel.

"Good," he says. "You're blocking my view."

The bus roars away, as a group of three push their way out through Tarzan's tinted glass doors, laughing and carrying on.

Is one of them... familiar?

Von stands, walks down the block to get a closer view.

Nah. False alarm.

This repeats just about every time somebody leaves. His perch is too far away—or his eyes are too messed up—but he can't very well just stand across the street, staring. Too obvious.

Finally, a familiar figure leaves Tarzan's, wearing a trucker cap.

Ah, yes, Von thinks. *The eternal trucker cap, Max's effort to hide his bald spot. Both vain and in vain.*

Von skips down the block. Traffic is sparse—but the drivers on the road at this hour are either speeding or drunk or both. He waits for his opportunity, and crosses as briskly as he can. His foot throbs with renewed zeal.

Max is oblivious. Probably walking in a boozy haze. He crosses through the main parking lot, to the parking lot of the neighboring brake-and-muffler garage. He's dug his car keys out of his jeans when Von calls out to him.

"Max!"

The man turns. It's him all right. Beady eyes set in a broad, flat face. Red cheeks, red nose, bushy blond beard. The eyes narrow even further. He comes to a stop by the driver's side door of a Toyota pickup; the yellow blinkers flash, in time with a sharp *chirp-chirp*. He reaches for the door handle.

Don't get in, Max. Don't be such a pussy.

"Max-a-million!" he says, as he leaves the sidewalk to close the distance, very aware now of his gimpy stride holding him back.

"Do I know you?" Max says, uncertain. He opens the door.

"It's your boy, Von!"

The squint turns into a frown. "Von?"

"Hell yeah, brother! What's good?"

"What are you—"

Smiling, Von crashes into the door, slamming it closed. He continues on, barreling into Max, pushing him into the wall of the pickup bed.

"The *fuck*—"

Von pulls the gun from his pocket, punches it into Max's stiff, unyielding paunch, then jams the barrel up under the man's chin. His beard is long enough to tickle Von's trigger finger.

"Do I have your attention, Max?"

"The fuck you want, Von? You fucking criminal."

"I'm more than just a criminal," Von says, through gritted teeth. His wrist is flaring up again. He'd anticipated punching a pillow, not a cinder block of belly fat. "I'm a killer. Remember that Max, as you answer this question. Because I'm only going to ask it once, and if you answer it wrong, I'm going to pull this trigger, and spray your brains all over your shitty pickup truck."

The bed is full of the sorts of things you'd expect from a landscaper: five-gallon buckets, gas cans, a weed-whacker, a leaf-blower, even a little generator. Looks like Max is running a side hustle.

"Ow."

"Ready, Max? This is your once-in-a-lifetime opportunity. And I mean that very literally."

"What the fuck, Von?"

"Where is Darnell?"

Nothing. Von pushes further upward, tilting Max's head back over the pickup bed. Aware that the pressure is probably keeping him from even being able to answer.

No answer.

He relents, just enough to allow Max to lower his chin, and open his mouth.

"Are those tears in your eyes, Max?"

"Come on, man."

"Don't '*come on man*' me—come on man you, bitch! What's next, you gonna piss yourself?"

"It hurts!"

The whole world has gone soft.

"How you think it's gonna feel if you make me pull this trigger?"

He jams the barrel up into his jaw again, straining his neck. Lifting him up onto tiptoes.

"Now, Max-a-million. I'm gonna ask you again. Where did Darnell and Shelly take my daughter?"

He lowers the gun, just enough.

"I swear to God, Von—I don't know."

"Bullshit, Max." Von pushes upward again.

"I'm telling you, man—I don't fucking know!"

"Don't make me pull this trigger, Max."

He smashes the cylinder into Max's ear. In doing so, though, he has given Max the opportunity to tuck his chin to his chest, and he's not budging.

Von presses the barrel into Max's cheek. Leans into him. Lowers his voice to a steely whisper.

"Last chance, Max."

"All I know is he quit his job, packed up a truck, and left."

"Better tell me something I don't already know, Max! Where did they go?"

"I don't know!" Panic lifts Max's voice an octave. Almost into a squeal. "What about the funeral, for his friend?"

"What about it?"

"He was from Gainesville. I think the funeral was today."

"Is that where they are? Max?"

Max nods, as slightly as he can, understandably not wanting to jar the pistol burrowed into the joint of his jaw. Von can tell he's lying, though. Just trying to save his miserable skin. He doesn't know shit.

"Fuck," Von says.

Suddenly drained of energy, as though all the adrenaline has left his body. His wrist is in agony. He lowers the gun, and steps back.

"Give me some money."

Might as well make this trip worth my while. What a waste of time.

"Jesus Christ, Von," Max says, rubbing his jaw with one hand, his chin with the other.

"Money, Max. Now."

"How much?"

"How ever much you think your life is worth, shit for brains."

Max cleans out his wallet.

"Forty-seven dollars?" Von says. "Remember that. That's how much your life is worth."

"Good Lord," Max says. "What the hell? You could've just asked."

"That was me asking nicely," Von says, as he turns to go. "If I find out you were lying—or if I hear you snitched on me—you'll see me when I'm not playing nice."

He stalks away through the parking lot. He's got a long walk ahead of him. He walked all the way here from Jasmine's, because when he left the building something told him not to drive. That little paranoid intuition.

The same intuition tells him to drop the phone, now. In case they get the number out of Howie and have some way of tracking him as a result. He tosses it into one of the omnipresent green dumpsters.

Can't trust nobody these days.

What's the world coming to? No loyalty anymore. The code of the streets? Gone. Everybody just fucks each other legally now, with contracts and insurance and interest rates and calling the cops when shit doesn't go your way.

The whole damn world has gone soft.

While he's walking, he has a revelation. A "come to Jesus" moment.

Darnell has eluded him. For the time being. Von has to concede that. Darnell's cowardice has saved his skin, if not his soul.

But he fears me—that much is clear. He should've feared me this much before I got out. Hell—as soon as I went in.

Should never have given me the chance to come find them in the first place.

If you think about it, so much of this is on him. Whether he was the one to rat me out or not.

Because if he'd respected me from the start, none of this would've happened. He would've cleared out of Naples—out of Southwest Florida entirely.

He's got the fear of God now, ain't he?

At least he's learned to fear Von Martin—which means he respects me. Like I said to Pastor Tom, this was never about revenge. This is about respect. Once I get my shit sorted, I'll be back. But through proper channels. Meantime, it's best for Tara if she has some stability. Last thing I would want is to damage her, or mess up her future somehow. Bad enough she's got my genes.

Thing is, that intuition is telling him Darnell wasn't the guy who set him up. Screaming at him.

He's just not that smart. He's not that ambitious. Once I went upstate, I bet it was Shelly coming around to him, making her interest known. She probably saw him as a sucker. A nice-guy provider type. She's probably the one who got him going back to school and changing jobs, just so he could make more money. Darnell always was the "go along to get along" type.

Raul, on the other hand.

Now there's a snake in the grass.

For Raul it wasn't a question of ambition. I didn't have anything he would want.

Except for the fact that I was getting away with shit, where he'd been busted. And I was running his crew for him, better than he ever could. So that made me look smarter. Not just to him, but to everybody.

And that's what he couldn't stand.

That's why he ratted me out.

Pride.

What's that line? About pride before the fall?

A lesson Raul needs to learn.

Along with respect.

When you don't set the record straight with the world, then that disrespect becomes one of those invisible-but-visible scars that you carry around with you, that makes you a target. Lets the rest of the world know you're a sucker. An easy mark.

Lord knows I ain't tryna bear that brand on my forehead the rest of my goddamn life.

CHAPTER
SIXTEEN

THE NEXT AFTERNOON, soon as Jasmine leaves for work, Von is out the door as well.

First stop: a sporting goods store, for some fresh drip that actually fits. Dark urban camo hunting pants with lots of pockets. A charcoal gray sun-shirt with long sleeves that he can roll up past his elbows. Splurges on some new Timbers, also black.

I'm only allowed out at night, might as well blend in.

A box of ammo for the .38.

That about cleans him out. If it wasn't for Max's contribution, he wouldn't have had enough.

After walking for a while on Vanderbilt, he stops in a diner. Treats himself to a house special: two eggs, two sausage patties, two pancakes, two hash browns, two slices of rye toast. Coffee, which he loads up with cream and sugar. Not because he likes it like that, but for the extra energy. He's going to need it.

He takes his time eating, scraping every last bit of yolk from the plate with the toast. Every time the waitress passes with the coffee pot, he nods. Each time he thinks maybe she'll ask whether he has a big night ahead, to which he will say, "I gotta put in a shift tonight," but she just fills his mug and leaves him to sip it in peace.

What she does say, when she comes around without the carafe and slips the check under his mug, is, "Not trying to rush you, hun." She clears the last of his plates. The sun is setting out over the gulf, and the place is starting to fill up; a crowd has gathered by the door, waiting for a table to clear.

He just smiles, and keeps sipping. Until there's nothing left, and it's clear she's not coming around with more.

He lays out the last of his cash, and heads back out into the dying light, and the fading heat.

By the time he's through the old part of town, and into the vacation homes, night has fallen. Von turns from Gordon and heads toward the inlet. Head on a swivel, eyes scanning side to side. He knows what he's looking for.

Eventually he finds it. A red single-seater kayak, on its side under a house, draining. Not locked up. A plastic oar leans against the wall next to it, a blade at each end. The house is dark; no cars in the driveway. He hoists the kayak up over his head, upside down, rests the seat on his crown, balances the backrest on his shoulders, grabs the oar in his right hand. A dog barks, but from inside a house on the other side of the street.

In no time he's crunched his way across the yard of crumbled sea shells and is standing at the water's edge. He lowers the boat from his shoulders and eases it into the water. The boots are indeed waterproof. The kayak wobbles as he gets himself situated, then he pushes from shore with the paddle and begins to row. He'll probably have blisters on his hands by the time he gets there—should've bought some gloves—but fuck it. He glides silently through the darkness. Clouds are gathering at the horizon, obscuring the rising moon.

The inlet's farther shore is shrouded in darkness, pines and mangroves crowded down along the water's edge. But he knows which set of docks he's looking for. Hell, he helped build them.

He swings the kayak in past Raul's boats, hugging the pilings, in the shadows.

Raul owns a deep-sea fishing boat, which Von was out on once, back in the day. Looks like he's added a new speedboat as well, low and sleek, with three Mercury 300s hanging off the stern.

He shoves the kayak up on the shore, turns it around so he can hop in for a quick getaway.

He contemplates the speedboat for a moment. Wouldn't he like to borrow *that*. Take it all the way down to the Keys, start all over again, fresh and new and clean. Allows himself a brief fantasy of freedom, the onrushing wind streaming his hair back. Putting all his problems behind him.

Hot-wiring was never his thing, though.

Besides—first up, he's got a job to do.

A promise to keep.

Not to Jasmine, or Shelly. Not even to Tara. A promise he made to himself. It's like Mr. Counselor Dude said: *You don't get respect from others until you respect yourself.* And you respect yourself by keeping your word to yourself. Following through on what you promised yourself you would do, in the privacy of your own heart, when nobody else is around. When you do what you set out to do.

Even when there is no immediate reward.

He who walks with the Lord lays up his treasure in Heaven.
Haha, mixing Pastor Tom with Mr. Counselor Dude.

He crouches low as he moves, covering behind the fish-cleaning station and the palmettos and the gazebo and finally the covered grill, waiting at each stopping point to see if there is any reaction from the brightly lit house. Nothing. They aren't expecting an approach from the sea side. He's hitting them from where they least expect it. He's the one picking the time, and the place.

He's considering his next move when a vehicle pulls into the driveway.

He straightens and runs through the open stretch of the backyard, reaches the corner. He's breathing heavy now, and sweating.

It's the Escalade. Could be Raul returning from dinner.

This is his chance. To set the record straight. To right the wrongs.

He leans his head around the corner of the house. The driver side opens, and Li'l Ern steps out, closes the door. He has a gun in his hand, and as he walks around the front of the car he makes a show of surveying the perimeter. Away from where Von is hiding.

He can't help but smile. He's blindsiding these fuckers. Hitting them with the sucker punch.

Li'l Ern opens the passenger door, and Raul steps down. Big Ern is walking down the steps to meet them.

Now—

Von steps around the corner, out into the open.

He sights down the barrel. Li'l Ern is in his way, but then he closes the door behind Raul, and there is his opportunity: Raul moves toward the stone steps, lifts his foot.

—or never.

"Raul!"

He has to know who's taking him down, or what's even the point?

He squeezes the trigger. Raul flinches. Li'l Ern whirls. Big Ern leaps down the steps.

Von squeezes again, and again. Raul ducks and sprawls over the steps. Flashes appear at Li'l Ern's head—he's shooting back now, walking back along the Escalade as he fires. A whine at Von's ear like an enormous mosquito as chipped fragments of stucco strike his cheek.

Big Ern covers Raul with his own body. Von squeezes the trigger again, and again.

Li'l Ern steps sideways, then spins and falls to the ground like a boulder fell out of the sky and flattened him.

Von aims again—the repeated kicks have lifted the gun, shifted his grip—at the body writhing beneath Big Ern. He squeezes the trigger. The bullet kicks up gravel in front of the bodies. Squeezes again, only to hear an empty click, with no kick back into his palm.

Reload. Then we'll get closer, to make sure.

He reaches into his pocket, and then there is a sensation in his lower leg like somebody took a car antenna and whipped him with it, right along the side of his calf. Instinctively he recoils, and bullets fall from his hand into the gravel at his feet.

Big Ern is still lying on top of Raul, but he's got a gun of his own out now, and Von sees the muzzle flash and he's sure that this one has his name on it.

He ducks back around the corner. His hands are shaking too much. He barely manages to swing the cylinder open, much less feed these finicky bullets into their chambers.

Goddamn it, Howie! Why couldn't you have gotten me a nine, with a proper magazine?

Another bullet punches right through the stucco near his head; he flinches, and more of his own bullets spill into the gravel at his feet.

Voices around the corner. Including Raul's. He peeks his head around. Big Ern is stooped at Li'l Ern, one hand on the sprawled body, the other still training the gun in Von's direction. He turns his head toward Von, straightens his lifted arm, and Von ducks back around the corner, chased by the rapid fire *bap-bap-bap* and more bullets whining and crashing into the wall.

He'd seen another man coming down the steps, though. And Raul scrambling on hands and knees toward the front of the Escalade. To hide, the coward.

"He's reloading!" He hears a voice say. Maybe Big Ern.

"Get that fucker!" That's Raul. *Leading from the rear, of course.* "Go after him!"

He's only managed to get one bullet chambered, when he hears feet running over gravel. He pushes away from the wall and takes off sprinting. Hasn't gone two steps, before he's down, sprawled in the gravel. The gun flies free from his hand, disappears in the grass.

That fucking leg! Good Lord that burns.

He pushes himself up, staggers forward. Searches through the grass till he finds his gun. Without even looking he fires back toward the corner where he stood.

The bang of his gun is followed by the sound of a body diving into gravel.

Give them something to think about, at least.

He takes off limping through the yard, toward the grill. He can reload there.

Once at the grill, he sees a man moving through the kitchen, who will have a clean shot at him. He continues running, through the blinding pain, back the way he came, past the gazebo, past the fish-gutting station and the coolers and the life preservers.

Reaching the kayak, he splashes through the water, then vaults in. Drops the gun into the sloshing puddle at his feet, steadies himself with the paddle and starts to dig the blades into the water.

Don't look back. Just fucking row.

Stroke after stroke. He reaches the end of the dock and keeps on going.

He hears shouts behind him, but not so close as the docks. Still stuck in the yard. He glances back over his shoulder. They are being cautious. They keep saying something that sounds like "ear." "Not here," maybe. Or "clear."

Then, quite distinctly, "Find him!" *Raul. Shit. Up and walking. Just my luck, again.* "I want that fucker dead!"

Von can't help but laugh. Despite it all.

I bet you do, Raul.

It's a nervous laugh, though. A giggle, even. Uncontrolled.

Shouldn't have drunk all that coffee.

The clouds have spread over the entire sky.

At least I get a bit of a break, he thinks.

Voices float across the water, but they are distant, indistinct. Lights have been lit along the dock, and two figures pace back and forth, pointing out toward the water. But since the lights aren't reaching him, they're more of a hindrance.

He keeps rowing until he is across the inlet. He turns into a gap, finds the shadows of a group of trees growing down along the water. He's safe. For now. For the moment.

Down below his knee, his pant leg is dark, and clinging wetly to his skin. Some of it is from when he ran out into the water with the kayak at his side. It's not only water, though.

He's been shot. A long slash through the outer side of his calf, through both the fabric and his muscle. Not the bone, though. It burns like acid, poured directly onto his flesh.

Grazed.

Coulda been worse. A lot worse.

Coulda caught one like Li'l Ern did.

Oh well. Kid had it coming to him.

He knew what he was getting into, working for a cowardly asshole like Raul.

I don't think I got him—not the one I was after. Best believe he fears me now, though.

And what's fear but respect?

He rows a little further until he finds a clearing, digs the kayak's nose into the rocks. Once on land, he turns back toward the dock. The lights are still lit, but the figures have disappeared.

"I'm coming for you, Raul!" he calls across the water, as loud as he can. "Best *believe*!"

One man runs back down into the light. Big Ern, maybe. Certainly not Raul. Von barges his way into the undergrowth.

Now you know the score, Raul.

Now *we're square.*

By the time he gets back to Jasmine's apartment, she is already home. She is sitting at the kitchen table, with the bottle of tequila out, a half-empty glass in front of her. There is food, untouched, in containers on the counter. Smells like tacos.

"Uh-oh," he says.

"You went out?" she says.

"I was going crazy in here." He hobbles his way back through the hallway to the powder room.

"What did you do now?" she asks. The chair scrapes against the floor. He closes the door and gingerly pulls his pants down, lowers the toilet lid and sits on it. The dried blood is like glue, tugging at the ragged trail the bullet has dug into his skin.

Just as he's peeling his pant leg down over his wound, she barges her way in, banging the door against his knee.

"Hey!" he calls out. "How about some privacy!"

"What is that?" She raises her hands to her mouth. "What happened? What did you do?"

"I ran," he says, as nonchalantly as he can. "And some asshole took a shot at me."

"A cop?"

"No!" he says, with a scoffing laugh. "Some guy tried to stick me up. I pushed him away and ran. Then he shot me."

"In the leg?"

"Good thing he was a terrible shot."

"There's blood everywhere!"

"No shit, Sherlock." He reaches for her hand towel.

"Not that one," she says. "I have others."

She disappears, returns, helps him hop on his good leg to the main bathroom, where he can stretch out on the floor. She proceeds to run one of the washcloths under warm water, and starts to dab it against his wound.

She also has a brown bottle of hydrogen peroxide, and another of rubbing alcohol.

"Use the brown one," he says. He leans back, and allows her to take care of him. He can flex his foot—with pain, but it's not like the calf muscle is destroyed. Once she's finished, he can see that the cut isn't even all that deep. There is a flap of skin that she has cleaned and folded back into place, which she secures with several of the butterfly bandages. She covers the cut with cotton makeup removal swabs, and then wraps gauze around his entire calf, secures it all with medical tape.

"Better than any hospital," he says. He sits up, leans his back against the vanity drawers. She sits on the toilet.

"What did you do?" she says.

He sighs. "Man," he says, "if there were a time and a place for a cigarette, this would be it."

"I want the truth, Von," she says. "I can take it."

"I told you," he says. "I was out for a walk, and some tweaker thought he could stick me up. I pushed him away and ran—next thing I know, I'm on the ground with this pain in my leg. I guess he got scared and took off."

She shakes her head, holds it in her hands. Sits upright, contemplates herself in the mirror. Touches a cotton swab to the makeup around her left eye.

"That's looking better," Von says. Which is true, the

bruising is fading. She's replaced the cloth bandage and tape at her temple with a single flesh-toned band-aid.

"Everybody was talking about the shooting at the club," she says.

Shooting?

"You mean Darnell's friend?" he asks.

She nods. "The cops were there. Asking about you. Again."

"Maybe we should check the news," he says.

She shakes her head. "What do you think I was doing for two hours, until you showed up?"

"Is it that late?"

The frosted window behind her head is no longer completely dark. *Yes, it is that late.*

"I just want to go to sleep," she says, as she stands up, and steps over his bare legs. In the bedroom, she continues her thought. "I just want to wake up and see that this has all been a really, really bad dream."

"You and me both, babe," he calls out.

He can barely bend his left knee now, and not just because of the tight bandage. Every muscle in his leg seems to have stiffened. He has to roll to his left side, place his right foot on the bath mat, grip the edge of the vanity and haul himself up to standing. He's already swallowed a couple of painkillers; he knocks out four more from the pill bottle and washes those down with a handful of water.

She is already in bed; the light is out. He climbs in and stretches out next to her.

"Bet you never slept with a guy on the news before," he says. He reaches for her, but she grabs his hand and throws it back at him.

"I'm not trying to start anything," he says.

She rolls over. In the faint light creeping in through the

edges of the heavy curtains, he can see that she's crying, in her shaking shoulders.

He can hear it in her cracking voice, too. "What did you do?" she pleads.

"I told you," he says.

"We're never going to get out of here, now, are we." It's not a question, though. It's a statement.

"Of course we are," he whispers. He touches her right cheek, her good cheek, wipes the tears away with his palm. "We're going to escape this shithole and live together forever."

He knows this is a lie. Of course it is. Obviously.

But he wants it to be true.

"Even you don't believe that," she says.

"My heart is in the right place," he says.

"But it's like you said, Von," she says. "It's not the words that count. It's the actions."

He rolls over onto his back, gingerly shifting his leg. Folds his hands behind his head.

"Just like a chick," he murmurs, "using your own words against you. They never forget, and they never let you forget."

"I love you, Von," she says.

"What?" He turns his head sharply toward her. The bed shakes slightly. "You fucking with me now?"

"See what I mean?" she says. She rolls onto her side, facing away from him.

"I'll give you some action over words," he says.

But he doesn't make a move. He just stares into the blackness hovering above him. Waiting for sleep to steal into the room and overpower him.

CHAPTER
SEVENTEEN

JASMINE WAKES him for a brief moment when she leaves the bed, but while listening to her rustling around in the bathroom he falls back asleep. When he finally does wake up and manages to lever himself out of the bed—his left leg aches and itches, the bandages dig into his flesh like claws—she is gone.

Leaning heavily on her bureau, then her couch, then the overstuffed armchair, he makes his way to the kitchen. Finds some instant coffee in the pantry, heats a mug of water in the microwave, then mixes the two. It's pretty awful, but with some cream and sugar it'll do till she returns with lattes from Starbucks, as she's been doing.

All out of cream, too. If he still had his phone he could text her, tell her to pick some up. She's probably aware, though.

All out of food, period. He eats a grapefruit. It leaves his mouth puckered, his gut curdled.

He checks the news. Immediately finds an anchor talking about the shooting in Bay Mar Estates, with a photograph of Raul's mansion, with sheriffs' SUVs and a squat fire department emergency vehicle parked on the pebble lawn. Cut to a picture of yellow tape cordoning off the scene around Raul's Escalade, with the passenger door hanging open. Cut to a close-up of all the little evidence tents on the ground, marking bullet casings.

"One man was killed, another man wounded in the shooting."

A picture of the deceased appears on the screen. "Ernesto Montevideo, 24. Driver and personal assistant to Mr. Gimenez."

Li'l Ern. Ain't that a bitch—catching a bullet for your boss. That's some serious bad luck—for you and me, both, man. I just can't catch a break.

"Wounded in the exchange of gunfire was Anthony Johnson, 36. Mr. Gimenez's chef and personal assistant." Followed by a picture of Big Ern.

How many "personal assistants" does this guy have?

Call it like it is: they're his bodyguards. Except he doesn't want the news to call them that, because then the world will see you for who you are, right Raul? A coward, hiding behind hired men. Because you don't have any friends anymore. You have to pay people to protect you now. You have to pay people to pretend to be your friends.

"Johnson was shot once in the arm, and is presently receiving treatment at North Naples Hospital and in stable condition."

Cut to Raul himself, wrapped in a blanket.

"I can't believe it," he says. He shivers. From the faint light and lack of direct sun Von guesses this was recorded much earlier in the morning. "Ernesto was a good friend. And now he's gone."

Lifting his eyes to the heavens, Raul stops. Wipes his eyes with the heels of his hands.

Then lowers his hands and stares directly into the camera.

As though he were trying to pierce into Von's very soul.

"He laid down his life for me," he says, "and I will never forget that. I am confident that justice will be served, on his behalf. And soon."

Von claps at the face on the TV screen.

"Bravo," he says, as he slowly claps. "Bra-vo! Break out the Academy Award. You may be able to fool these clowns. You may be able to fool the rest of the goddamn world. But you can't fool me, bro. I see right through your shit."

Besides—crying? Tears? On TV? Have some dignity.

He shakes his head. *Have some self-respect.*

And now his two goons are out of the picture. Now would be the perfect time to catch him—but he knows he can't leave the apartment. Not now. Not with all this heat.

Von is no longer a "person of interest." He is now the sheriff's "chief suspect."

But what are they saying about me?

The reports describe him as a disgruntled former employee of Mr. Gimenez, recently released from prison after serving a four-year term for Petty Theft. A crime he committed during an evacuation order.

Von winces. That makes him seem so... *small-time.*

Of course they bring it up without any context.

First of all, the original charge was Grand Theft, but his jailhouse lawyer pleaded it down. Third Degree, but still: Grand Theft. Not Petty.

Second, and most important: that evacuation order hadn't even gone into effect yet, not when he was in the place. But since they purposely *delayed*, and brought him in and processed him *after* the order took effect, that mandated max sentencing.

Should've contested it, he thinks. *Should've fought it all the way. That was some serious bullshit. If I'd had the money to hire a decent attorney...*

They are only showing the jailhouse pic of him now.

Sure. Make sure everybody knows I'm a con. Not a family man—bet they won't even mention that. No, of course not—because I no longer am, legally.

Thanks for that, Shelly.

Makes me sick, Raul going on about "justice being served." If there was any justice in the world...

Lying on the sofa, left leg elevated on a pillow, he watches the coverage on the local news. But as the day wears on, the reports repeat. Eventually the news gives way to talk shows and soap operas and game shows. He's channel-surfing and intermittently dozing.

Law and Order.

People's Court.

Judge Judy.

He's on the stand. The cameras are on him, now. His turn to make his case. To set the record straight.

I'm a man from a different era. I'm a throwback. I'm old school.

I come from a time when loyalty meant something.

I used to look up to this man, like a father. He was like the father I never had.

Don't get it twisted: I ain't asking for any sympathy on that score. Everybody's got their problems. Life ain't easy. I ain't never asked for a handout. Never asked for any charity.

There is a tear or two in the gallery. Among the women.

There was a time when I would've been Li'l Ern. He thumps his chest. *When I would've been the one to catch a bullet for this guy.*

This man—he points toward Raul in the front row of the audience—*this so-called man wants to turn his back on where he came from. Turns his back on the people who helped him get to where he is. Now that he has some money, all of a sudden he's better than us. He's left us behind.*

I would never be like that. I would never change, no matter how much money I had.

The whole world has gone soft.

A few of the men in the audience are nodding along now. The old heads.

They get it. They've been there.

I come from a time when your word meant something. When you gave your word, and you didn't have to sign your name on a contract. Or summarize your life on a so-called resume. Because what is any of that anyway? Just words, on a piece of paper.

I come from a time when you were judged by your actions, not your words.

When you had a crew, not a corporation.

When you lived by the law of nature, not the law of the land.

Because I'm old school.

And if that's a crime, then I'm guilty as charged.

The audience is on its feet now, all but Raul, who can do nothing but hang his head low.

People around the country—watching in their living rooms and on their phones—they, too, are on their feet.

The judge—damn if he doesn't look like Pastor Tom—is banging his gavel, calling for order. But even he has to recognize that Von isn't just another case—he's become a *cause*. The little people—the poor people—they see themselves in him. He's striking a blow for them.

I speak for the little people, Von says, on his feet now, gripping the witness stand like it was a pulpit. The people surge toward him, despite the bangs of the gavel, the futile attempts of the bailiff to restrain them.

I speak for those who have never gotten any respect, their entire lives. That's what this whole crusade has been about:

respect. Not revenge. Never revenge. Revenge is petty. Revenge is driven by emotion.

This movement—OUR movement—is bigger than that. Our guiding light, our north star has always been the same. We only want one thing from this world:

Respect.

And we're going to demand it. We're going to make sure we get it.

The studio audience lifts him up, to their shoulders, and carries him from this phony cardboard and plywood courtroom, to freedom.

Their hero.

Von Martin.

―――

When Von wakes, Jasmine is sitting on the overstuffed armchair. Perched on the edge of the seat cushion. Near his head. The windows are dark; the television is dead. The only light comes from the lamp on the end table, between them and above.

She's not crying, not now, but her smeared mascara and disheveled mop of hair tell him that she has been. Downturned lines seem etched around her mouth and her eyes, as though her face has been frozen into a rictus of sadness and despair.

Not exactly what you want to wake up to. Not after such a nice dream...

He doesn't need to ask. She's seen the news. She knows about Raul.

She knows he's a killer.

But she's here, right? She hasn't turned him in, or he'd have gotten an even more rude awakening.

"You've been lying to me," she says.

He sits up, carefully shifts his injured leg from the couch to the coffee table.

"What are you talking about?"

"This!" She waves her phone at him. "On the news!"

"Look," he says, voice calm, tone measured. "I was going after Raul, and this other guy got in the way. It's a shame, but that's the way it happened. I can't go back and change the past."

"Raul?" The lines around her eyes deepen, even as her eyes widen. She looks absolutely crazy. *Lack of self-control.* "Who the fuck is Raul?"

"He's the one who set me up to take the fall."

"He was your boss!"

Von widens his own eyes, and thrusts his finger toward her. "I did four years because of him, and then he wants to act like he doesn't even know me? You see how I couldn't let that stand, right? You see how that's one of those invisible scars I was talking about, that broadcasts to the world, 'this guy is a sucker, this guy is a patsy, he'll take the fall for anybody. He'll do a bid of four years and not say a word.'"

"You were stealing," she says. "And you got caught. Not everything is a big conspiracy against you, Von."

"Is that so? I guess their little news reports don't mention that he's a criminal, just like me—no, they don't want to let you know that he's done time, too. Because they want to paint me as the villain."

"You tried to kill him! You killed another man instead! That makes you the villain!"

"What am I supposed to do? I mean, you see how I had to teach him respect, right? If I don't, then who is ever going to respect me again?"

"Just take that gun and shoot me, too," she says. "You might as well. You're going to, anyway, aren't you? To make sure there aren't any witnesses, or some shit? You fucking psycho."

Her voice is rising into a shrill screech. *No self-control whatsoever.*

"I'd never let anyone hurt you," he says, as calmly as possible. 'Psycho' hurts—*that's uncalled for*—but he's willing to let it slide.

"This is hurting me!" she says. "Can't you see that?"

"You're not involved," he says.

"But I am involved! You involved me!"

"You invited yourself in!" he says. He clears his throat, restrains his own rising tone.

Breathe in—breathe out. Calm. Self-control.

"You were bored, you were lonely, you wanted a change of scenery. Hell if I know why. But you knew I was trouble. You always did. Don't deny it."

She buries her head in her hands, sobbing. Then she's gasping for air. She stands up, fanning her face with her hands. Sits back down. Stands back up. Still gasping. Her mouth opening and her cheeks swelling and deflating like she's a goldfish in a bowl.

"I'm having—a panic—attack," she says, through chattering teeth.

He stands, despite the pain in his leg, and grabs her by the shoulders. Wraps his arm around them, walks her toward the balcony doors. For fresh air.

She shakes her head, digs her heels into the carpet. "No," she says. "No!"

"Okay," he says. "Okay."

What's she think, I'm going to throw her off? And she calls me a psycho.

He turns her around, guides her back to the armchair, sits her down. Leans her back into it. Takes a position behind the chair and begins to rub her shoulders.

"Come on, babe," he says, kneading his knuckles into her tightly tensed muscles. "We'll get out of this yet."

She flops her hands open down along her thighs. "How, Von?" she demands. She looks up at him. Her upside-down face, wrenched with distress, is even more hideous than it was before. Her breasts sag beneath her halter top like deflated balloons. "How are we ever going to get out of this?"

"I've hit an unlucky streak," he says. "I'll admit. But any pro will tell you: keep doubling down. If you keep doubling down, no matter how long that unlucky streak lasts, eventually your luck will turn around, and then *bam*—you're right back to even money."

"You're not making any sense, Von!"

He shrugs. "That's just math."

She sits in silence, chin nearly on her chest, while he keeps rubbing her shoulders.

"You don't even know my real name," she says. "All this time, you've only called me Jasmine."

"So?" he says. "I like Jasmine."

"You don't even remember, do you? When I told you my real name?"

He remembers her making a big deal about telling him, one night back in the day when they were flirting, back when he and Shelly were just dating. He remembers persuading her to tell him. Remembers thinking that he could have her, easy, if he wanted.

"Of course I do," he says.

But he didn't want her then. What he wanted then was somebody stable. Somebody who would be good for him long-term, not just good to him for a week or two. Somebody whose job wasn't to flirt and talk dirty with other men right in front of his face. How would that be showing any respect?

"Do you, Von?"

He leans forward, and kisses the top of her head. The scent

of her scalp—a salty smell, like sweat, or tears, or even blood—fills his nostrils.

"Nora," he whispers.

Her shoulders slump. "You remembered," she sobs.

For once, he doesn't blurt out what he's thinking. The truth. Seeing it in sharpie on the takeout container.

He straightens, and continues kneading her shoulders. Begins working his way down, toward her breasts.

Just another hopeless romantic.

CHAPTER
EIGHTEEN

HE WAKES WHEN JASMINE—*NORA*—LEAVES the bed and heads for the bathroom. Tempted as he is to fall back asleep, he forces himself to his feet, makes his way to the kitchen. This morning, he's going to make the eggs and bacon. It's the least he can do. He's starting to feel like he's in her debt. Needs to find a way to balance that out.

When she finally does emerge, the eggs have cooled, the bacon grease congealed. She's dressed and ready to go out. She's not hungry.

"You know what I've been thinking?" he asks. "While I was out here cooking breakfast for you?"

"I have no idea what goes on in that head of yours."

"Well—do you want to know?"

"Enlighten me."

"Thought of the day: you know how in the movies, the main character spends the whole movie chasing after the smokeshow, right? Meanwhile, there's the good girl, who's like his sidekick. She's not ugly, but she's dorky. Big glasses, always wears her hair up. She's got substance, but the other one's got style, right? He's after the one with the looks, but she's all superficial. But it's only at the end that he finally realizes, that the real one was right there, under his nose, all along. And then the mousy geek takes off her glasses and lets down her hair, and turns out she's a total dime, and the music kicks in and they kiss and live happily ever after?"

"Where's this going, Von? I gotta—"

He steps toward her, grabs her elbows; her arms are folded over her chest. She flinches, but doesn't pull away.

"I thought I was so smart, back in the day. I thought I was skipping to the end of that movie, and cutting out the hour and a half of bullshit. I thought I had the good girl, just because she wore glasses and had a nine-to-five and wanted a family."

Her eyes can't seem to find a place to settle. They rove from the fridge to the countertop to the floor. Anywhere but meeting his own.

"But then when the chips are down," he continues, "look who turns out to be a terrible person, and look who actually got the goods. Look who actually sticks by you."

He pulls her to him, wraps his arms around her, even though hers remain folded over her chest.

"Turns out it was the hot stripper I should've been after all along," he whispers.

His lips seek hers. She returns his kiss, but briefly. A chaste peck.

He releases her, waves with a flourish toward the door. He's not trying to keep her here against her will.

"Just something that's been messing with my mind these last few days."

"Words, Von," she says, at the door. "Nice words—but just words."

That stings—but she's right.

"You're not the main character." She opens the door, steps over the threshold. "And I'm nobody's sidekick."

"Going to get lattes?" he asks. But the heavy door slams shut behind her.

She ain't coming back.

This doesn't rise to the level of conscious thought—these aren't words that he formulates in his brain. It's an instantaneous certainty born from the evasiveness of her eyes, the tone of her voice, the set of her shoulders.

A conviction that surges up from deep within.

Ain't that a bitch, he thinks. *Well, you tried. Tried to express yourself. Tried to let her know how you feel. Tried to be vulnerable, like Mr. Counselor Dude would recommend.*

Should've known better than to get all gushy, like a simp.

Soon as it's dark, we're getting the hell out of here.

He cleans his wounds, changes his bandages. He flips through channels, losing himself in the flickering on the screen but without really absorbing any of what he is seeing. He pulls another book down from her shelf, but catches himself reading the same paragraph over and over again. The thoughts crowd in, and there is no room for anything else to enter.

Time has begun to blur, and smear.

Just as it used to, for long stretches, upstate.

He stands up, and paces the apartment, a gimpy tiger.

It wasn't even that bad, inside, he thinks. *Maybe that's where I belong. Maybe I need that structure—that discipline imposed upon me—to be the best version of myself.*

He can't pace for too long before the leg starts to bother him, or the foot, and he has to sit. Or lean. Out on the balcony, he rests his forearms on the balcony railing. The marina is quiet today.

When you start thinking like this, he thinks, *that's when you know they got to you. They've convinced you that you're a bad person. That you're defective, somehow. That you don't belong out here, with them. In the general pop.*

Fuck that. Fuck them.

There's a whole great big world out there, bro. There's a place for you in it.

You could hop on a boat and sail toward that horizon, and you'll never reach it. You could just keep on sailing, forever.

He notices the three white SUVs lined up in the fire lane below at the same time he hears a muffled voice through the apartment door: "Naples County Sheriff! Search warrant! Open up!"

He's about to close the door behind him when he spots the gun resting on the coffee table. His wounded leg burns as he tiptoes back into the living room. Sharp, purposeful voices from out in the hallway end with a key rattling in the lock. He grabs the gun, limps back to the balcony.

The front door opens with a bang, followed by heavy footsteps.

"Naples County Sheriff! Search warrant!"

He recognizes Alvin's gruff drawl. As he slides the balcony doors closed behind him as quietly as possible, another man's voice calls out, "Kitchen clear!"

The balcony is small, maybe eight feet by twelve. A metal railing tops the waist-high concrete wall; to his left, a partition separates this balcony from the neighbor's—also concrete, about seven feet tall. He leans around the partition—the neighboring balcony contains two metal chairs, a small circular café table, a covered grill. The doors are closed, curtains drawn.

Thirteen floors up. Fourteen, whatever. Long way down.

Muffled voices move closer to the living room.

Move. Now.

He climbs up onto the railing, his right wrist protests as he grips the metal bars; his injured leg barely supports his weight. He swings his body around the partition, and for a terrifying moment he hangs over the abyss, the tiki huts around the pool down below tiny dollhouses.

His right foot, still sore, finds purchase on the neighbor's railing. The smooth concrete provides no handholds, his grip comes from the pressure of his hands, one on either side of the wall, squeezing toward each other. As he shifts his weight around the partition, his right wrist gives way. His right foot lands on one of the chairs, but as he leans onto it, his left leg catches in the corner formed by the railing and the partition, causing him to lose his balance. He flails his arms out as the chair kicks out from under him and his chest crashes into the grill, forcing the air from his lungs.

Smooth.

Sucking for air as quietly as he can, he lowers himself from the grill, sits down behind it, bends his knees to his chin. His left calf burns, the fresh bandages pulling and stretching with every movement.

"Check the balcony!" Alvin's voice rings through the glass doors.

"Balcony clear," comes a voice from Jasmine's balcony.

"You sure?"

Footsteps on the balcony next door. The scrape of her lounge chairs being kicked aside. Making sure he's not hiding underneath.

"Just the usual balcony shit."

A fainter voice, from inside: "Bedroom clear!"

Von wraps his arms around his shins, hugs them to him, making himself as small as possible. His leg is throbbing now, and he can feel something wet and warm spreading down his calf. The wound has opened up again.

"Check the neighbors," Alvin's voice carries out to the balconies.

"No sign."

More footsteps, this time heading back inside. Von stays frozen behind the grill, not daring to move. A trickle of blood tickles his ankle.

"Search the rest of the building," Alvin's voice fades as he moves away from the balcony. "Check the stairwells."

The doors slide closed.

Von waits, counting his heartbeats, trying to gauge how long he should stay hidden.

A shiny crimson pool grows on the concrete around his bare heel. The deep, throbbing ache makes him dizzy.

After what feels like an hour but is probably only ten minutes, he hears the apartment door slam.

He waits another five minutes, then carefully peers around the edge of the grill. Nothing.

He claws at the grill cover with his left to lever himself up to standing. He nearly passes out from the pain as blood, trapped by his bent knees and hips, surges down toward his foot again. The apartment behind him is dark, no signs of life. He staggers over to the balcony railing, leans heavily upon it. The pool, the walkways, the parking lot—the SUVs still clustered around the building entrance. He retreats into the shadows.

Can't swing back over to Jasmine's yet. Too risky.

Shouldn't stay here either. Owner could come home any minute. If they aren't home already.

And I'm bleeding all over their balcony.

He limps to the sliding door and gently tests the handle. Locked, of course.

Nothing to do but wait. Wait until dark.

He sits heavily in one of the chairs. Swings his leg up onto the café table, to keep it elevated. Doesn't seem to be helping much, though.

Now would be a good time for a cigarette, he thinks. *A cigarette—and a bottle of tequila.*

He's going to have to swing back over that railing, sooner or later. And hope they didn't lock the sliding door behind them.

What are the odds of that? Fifty-fifty?
Sure—heads, they win. Tails, you lose.

The SUVs are gone. The sky above is tinged purple; below the orange lamps have flickered on, creating little islands of light among the sea of parked cars. He props one of the neighbor's chairs in the corner by the balcony wall and the partition, slowly raises himself to the railing and swings around the dividing wall, eases himself down to Jasmine's balcony. Not being in a terrified rush makes it seem so much easier.

The door is unlocked. *Finally I catch a break.*

He leaves the lights off as he moves around in the evening gloom. He's eaten everything in the house. Leftovers from the back of the fridge. Her pantry was never well stocked to start with. He's famished.

And he has no money. He searches through the kitchen drawers, through her bureau, through the pockets of her clothes hanging in the closet. He riffles the pages of all of her books, thinking of his own emergency stash in his father's Bible. Even checks the cracks and crevices of the couch and the armchair.

Nothing. Not even a single dollar bill. Not even a quarter.

Who lives like this? No food, no money—so close to the bone?
Well, not gonna lie—I been there, too.

In the bathroom, he turns on the lights. Has to see if he's going to redo his dressings. He douses the bullet trace with more foaming and hissing hydrogen peroxide, rewraps it as tightly as he can, painfully aware of how much more difficult this is without Jasmine's aid. He runs out of butterfly bandages and the gauze wrap before he can do the same with his wrist. He retightens the velcro straps on the brace—that will have to do.

He investigates her walk-in closet a little more thoroughly. This light he can turn on as well—no windows to worry about. Had there been a suitcase on that upper shelf? Are those gaps in the hanging clothes a little too conspicuous? Did she somehow manage to pack a bag, or even two, without him noticing? He can't be one hundred percent sure.

Clever girl.

Should've known she'd skip first chance she got.

Bruh—you DID *know. You went in with your eyes wide open, but then you closed them. What was it you said to her? Ignorance is bliss? Well, this wasn't ignorance. This was* ignoring. *Ignoring all her red flags.*

She played you, he tells himself. His shoulders shake, and his raspy laugh rings harsh—alien, even—in the empty room. *You're no better than her, dude.*

A hopeless romantic.

He pulls on his boots. Borrows clean shorts and a clean Hawaiian shirt from her ex.

Probably who she's with right now, he thinks. *Running to this clown, with her sob story. And with the bruises to back it up. Make it seem like her new man beat her—not just once, on the reg. He'll feel sorry for her, take her in. Give her a hug. Pour her a drink. Tell me more, tell me all about your hardships. One thing leads to another, and next thing you know—oops, how did that happen? How did we wind up in the bed? You just make me feel so safe, and comfortable, in your big strong arms.*

And so yet another man bends the knee. I dub thee Sir Save-a-ho, the White Knight.

A pat on the head with the same sword that, one day, when you least expect it—when you most need her—she's going to plunge into your belly, and twist those guts of yours all around.

Who cares. Time to go.

Where though? Away, for now. Away is good enough.

Gun in his shorts pocket, he makes his way down the

steps, leaning heavily on the railing, keeping his weight off his left leg.

Should've taken the elevator, he thinks.

Not so much because of the leg, which isn't so bad—so long as he's keeping most of his weight off it.

It's more so he could maintain the fiction that he was coming down from the fourteenth floor. But in the stairwell, each landing has the number of floors remaining to exit helpfully stenciled in black on the whitewashed cinder blocks. Each landing letting him know that he's been living these past days on the thirteenth floor, not the fourteenth.

No wonder my luck's been so shit.

Eyes wide open, though. No more of this willful ignorance.

No more pretending. This is real life, Von. Right here. Right now.

At the ground floor, he cracks open the stairwell door. The lobby is empty except for the security guard behind the desk, who's fiddling with his phone. Von waits until the elevator lets out a group of geezers; he slips from his doorway, walks along beside them.

Outside, he stays in the shadows, moves away from the building as quickly as his injured leg will allow. The sheriffs' SUVs are gone. Music from the tiki bar drifts through the parking lot. Life has returned to normal.

He makes it to the tree line that borders the marina, then stops to catch his breath.

Free. Still free.

But for how long?

And where the hell am I supposed to go now?

He starts walking through the parking lot—slowly—doing his best to disguise the limp, the angular solidity of his piece rhythmically bouncing against his thigh. His foot isn't too bad —the boots laced up tight seem to be helping. But the leg—

holy shit. He hates the way the shorts expose his homemade bandages.

But he's alive. As long as he's alive, there's still a chance.

Keep moving, he tells himself. *Just keep moving.*

Behind him, the lights of Delasol Views twinkle in the darkness, no longer a sanctuary but a trap he barely escaped. Beyond the marina stretches the golf course, then the main road, then... *what?*

Where?

By the time he gets to Tarzan's, he is famished, and sweating, and limping, and cursing the rotten luck that has gotten him to this place.

He walks in the door. The place is bustling. He finds a seat at the end of the bar. Orders a burger and a beer from the bartender that served him before. When the guy asks him if he wants to start a tab, he says, "Remember me? I'm Howie's friend." But the guy shakes his head.

"Cash, then," Von says. "At the end."

The asshole stares at him. Looks like he wants to say something, but then turns away, takes his order back to the kitchen.

Next thing he knows, Howie is at his shoulder. He wedges his bulk in between Von and his neighbor, pushing Von's stool sideways. Leans down over Von.

"Von," he whispers. "The fuck you doing here?"

"Ordering some food, man."

"Are you insane?"

"What? I'm hungry."

"You can't be here, man."

"I could really use a friend right now," Von says.

"I've been a friend," Howie says. "You can't say I haven't."

Von nods. Howie signals to the bartender. Says, "A burger, in a to-go box. Chop chop."

"With fries," Von says. "Extra fries."

The bartender turns and walks away. Von calls after him, "Don't forget the ketchup!"

"The fuck are you thinking?" Howie says.

"He forgot the ketchup last time."

"I mean, attacking a guy like Raul," Howie says, voice low. Urgent. "In Bay Mar! What did you think was going to happen? Like, what was your best-case scenario?"

"He had it coming," Von says. "He betrayed me, man. He ratted me out. You know I can't let that shit stand."

He can feel Howie staring at him. Like he wants to bore a hole in his head.

"When the food comes out," Howie says, "you have to go. And you can't be coming back, man."

"Fine." Von raises his hands. "Be like that."

Howie's belly brushes past his shoulder, and then he's gone. Von sips his water. Makes eye contact in the mirror with some dude down at the other end of the bar, whose eyes drop immediately.

Von stands, heads back to the bathrooms. He needs to take a leak. But he also needs to make sure.

The guy is wearing a polo shirt. In a joint where everybody's wearing a designer tee or a button-down print. The guy signals for the check.

Nah, Von thinks. *Nice try.*

Instead of the bathrooms, he pushes through a door labeled "Private." Heads up the stairs, down the hall that takes him over the lounge, and through another door. Into Howie's office. Howie lifts his head from a mirror—one line down, another waiting. Von recognizes the fear in his face—the panic —but Von isn't here for him.

"The cops are already here, Howard," he says, as he hobbles past. "Thanks for letting me know, asshole."

He reaches the window, hauls the cord that lifts the venetian blind, raises the sash. With his two hands making a cradle under his hamstring, he lifts his left leg up and through, and then he's out onto the low roof. At the edge, he lowers himself to his belly, throws his legs over the side, and does his best to lower himself down. The gutter is in the way, the metal creaking and protesting, and it pops free as soon as he shifts his weight fully onto it, but he grabs the sagging aluminum half-pipe and rides it down to the ground as another bracket pops free, then another. He still hits hard, and since he can only really use his right leg to land, he tilts backward and lands on his ass, smacks the back of his head on the ground. But he's up and moving, blinking away the stars, back past the dumpsters and into the undergrowth, till he reaches the parking lot of the Waffle House.

Keeps on walking. Never looking back.

Still hungry, sure.

But still free.

CHAPTER
NINETEEN

HE IS surprised to find cars in the church parking lot. Not many, a half-dozen or so. Even on Sunday, there had only been maybe twice this number. The blue Saturn is there, though the smile that he drew there with his own blood has been washed away. *Blood is no more permanent than sweat,* he supposes. *Or tears.* No more permanent than any of those traces we may leave behind as a sign of our efforts.

They have gathered in a circle around the side of the church, standing, holding hands, and the golden late-day sun slants in among them, tracing dust motes and gnats swirling in the air just above this henge of people. They are singing. Lifting up their voices.

"Join us, brother."

Pastor Tom breaks free from the circle and crosses the dusty earth toward him. A woman, equally ancient, also separates from the group and approaches Von with a beatific smile. They take up positions, one on either side, a hand on each of his elbows, a strange parody of the way the sheriffs grabbed him and hauled him off to the back of their SUV, and while he flinches at the memory, and recoils at the cringiness of being asked to join a group of the faithful singing hymns, and even though it would be so easy to free himself from their bony clutches, and despite the repulsiveness of their touch, the backs of their hands so mottled and veiny and skeletal—regardless of all of this internal clamor urging him to shake his head and dig in his heels—they lead him like one who is completely powerless, utterly in their thrall, to join their circle. They shift their hands from his elbows down into his hands, and as the circle opens, and shifts, they give their free hands to their neighbors, and the circle is once again complete.

Von doesn't know the words to any of the songs. He doesn't know who is choosing them. Is it Pastor Tom? Is it a program that they have agreed upon earlier? Are they practicing for something? Or is this simply something they are doing for fun? Well, not for fun, he guesses. To save their souls. That doesn't sound fun.

He stands there, silent. Aware that he is glowering, especially with the sun in his eyes, causing him to lower his head. He closes his eyes, even. But then that makes him feel dizzy, and he feels Tom's hand clamp down with surprising strength on his own hand, and another hand at his elbow, supporting him.

"Easy, there," Pastor Tom whispers.

No, wait—he does know this song. He moves his lips, says the words more than sings them:

"'Tis a gift to be simple, 'tis a gift to be free."

A gentle pressure on his right hand draws his attention to his diminutive, silver-haired neighbor, who smiles up at him through glasses that curve into sharp talon-like points at her temples.

"'Tis a gift to come down, where we ought to be."

He can't help but return her smile. Can't help but sing out a little more loudly now. Caught up in the infectious, communal joy.

"And when we find ourselves in the place just right—"

Joy—and nostalgia. He's not just remembering, he's reliving the time when he was a boy, standing in a similar circle, inside this very church, back when it was whole, and functioning. The children formed a smaller loop in the middle, his mom and dad stood with the rest of the adults in a ring around them. Sometimes they would move clockwise, while the adults moved counterclockwise, and vice versa, and it gave him the impression that they were all part of this geared machine that was rotating the entire church—hell, the entire world—and propelling it up on a giant screw, up toward Heaven.

"Twill be in the valley of love and delight."

The words pour out of him now, effortlessly, and they almost bring tears to his eyes. Love and delight. He sure could use some of that, right about now.

But the song isn't over. He's starting to regret his enthusiasm now, as he realizes he doesn't remember the next line, or lines. He watches the singing mouths around him, waits to hear the words enunciated, tries to follow along, tries to allow the words to flow through him from that deeper, unconscious part of him, but it's an effort again, and he just doesn't remember. Except he remembers that this was how church felt to him, most of the time—church, and school, and little league. Hell, all of life itself. Like he was always listening to hear what he should be saying, always watching to see what he should be doing, yet always off by half a beat or so. Always fighting to find that rhythm that seems to come so naturally to all these people.

Which is why this shit feels so cringe to him in the first place. Which is why he shouldn't have let these olds drag him into this nonsense.

"I've had enough love and delight, I think." He shakes his hands free. "I gotta sit down."

Pastor Tom searches for his eyes, briefly, but Von turns away, toward the trailer. Pastor Tom reaches for the woman's hand, and the circle closes once again behind him.

Von limps his way across the patchy lawn. Climbs up into the trailer.

He removes the revolver from his pocket and clunks it down on the Formica, works his way in behind the table and eases himself down onto the bench, head beneath the air conditioner. Which is silent, as the evening is blessedly cool.

He kicks off his heavy boots and when they hit the floor with a thud he remembers his new black camo pants and shirt. He left them back at Jasmine's, and he curses himself for making such a big mistake. They were an essential part of his plan: make his way north, stick to the back roads, travel by night, rest during the day. It isn't much of a plan. He just hasn't had the time to come up with a better one yet. And now, without the camo, with his bandages there for all to see, he feels exposed. Worse than naked: Jasmine's stupid ex's brightly billowing Hawaiian shirt feels like he might as well be wearing an enormous target on his back.

How could you be so stupid? Just one more way you self-sabotage—

Pastor Tom steps up and into the trailer.

"Do you have anything to eat?" Von asks.

"You're welcome to join us," Pastor Tom says. "We're having a potluck. People are bringing it from their cars."

"Maybe if there's anything left over," Von says.

It's not that he doesn't have the strength to get his ass up off the bench, tired as he is. No—he doesn't have the strength to make small talk with people he doesn't know. Or, worse—much worse—answer questions from people he doesn't know, but who *do* know him, who will want to pinch his cheeks or clap him on the back and say "I remember you when you were a little boy!"

"Join us," Pastor Tom says. "It will do you a world of good."

"I'm too tired," Von says. "I just want to go to sleep."

He turns over, faces the brown vinyl back of the bench, lays his head in the crook of his arm.

"When you turn your face away from your problems, you also turn your face away from your Father," Pastor Tom says.

"What do you know about problems, Pastor Tom?" Von asks.

"My name is not Tom," the old man says.

Von pivots his body around to face his host, careful not to roll off the narrow bench. "No shit?"

Pastor Tom shakes his head.

"Who are you, then?"

"My name is Job," Pastor Tom says.

"Wow," Von says. He's pretty sure the crazy old coot is fucking with him. Or just being crazy. "And all this time I thought you were that preacher my father liked."

"Go to sleep, then," the old man says, as he lowers himself back out of the trailer. "For the restless, sleep is a glimpse of Heaven."

Von grunts in reply. The screen door bangs shut, leaving him in the gathering gloom as the sun reddens and drops toward the tree line.

He tries to sleep, but the olds are out there gabbing and laughing while they eat. He remembers his father, how he would stand out there talking for what seemed like forever, while Von sat in the back of the church, reading.

Maybe he has slept, maybe not. The trailer is dark, though a few murmurs from beyond still filter into his consciousness. For some reason he remembers holding his daughter in his arms when he and Shelly brought her home from the hospital. She's been that throbbing in his foot, that bullet in his leg, that glass in his wrist, this entire time.

I made a mess of things, Tara, he thinks.

He directs his thoughts to her. *Which makes it a prayer, of sorts*, he supposes. He hopes. *As much a prayer as any other: hoping that the person you're praying to is somehow going to hear it, or answer it. Or believe it.*

"I fucked things up royally, didn't I, Tara," he murmurs into the cracking vinyl cushion. "But always remember, girl, and never doubt—I did it all for you."

The air conditioner begins rattling, and wheezing, and blasting its frigid breath down over his head. The trailer is full of light. Von levers himself up to a sitting position. Pulls on his boots. The old man is nowhere to be seen, but there are plastic containers and crockery on the table, loosely covered with tin foil or plastic. A couple of breaded chicken drumsticks, some sort of vegetable casserole, cannelloni stuffed with cheese, a flat dish of what looks like brownies except they're savory, with chunks of sausage and potatoes in a mixture of eggs and cheese and bread. A veritable feast! He eats his fill. And then some.

As he reaches for the sheet of crumpled foil that had covered the cannelloni, he reveals his father's Bible, hidden beneath.

Know what? he thinks. *I'm gonna sign my name in there. It's been a hell of a week.*

I didn't get all of them who definitely deserved to get got. I'll admit that. I'll own that. I take full accountability for that.

Darnell, he got away.

Raul, too.

But that was down to luck, more than anything. The effort was there. The intent was there. The actions—not just words.

And they both fear me now, don't they? Oh, yeah—best believe those fuckers fear me.

That's respect. And what did I say, right at the outset of all of this? Soon as I got out? First thing?

I ain't about revenge. I'm all about respect.

So, I don't know if Pops would agree with me. In fact, I'm pretty sure if he were here he'd be yelling at me, telling me what all I did wrong, and how I should've done this instead of that, and how I need to be doing this now, and why haven't I thought about that.

I'm sure, to his eyes, I did everything wrong, and fucked everything up.

But ain't that part of being a man? Part of being grown?

Making your own mistakes—but also knowing deep down, in your heart of hearts, that you did what you could. Like Mr. Counselor Dude would say: you did the best you could, with the limited resources you had available to you at that time. And that's exactly what I did.

When you know that's true, then it doesn't matter what anybody else says to you. Not even your father. Who art in Heaven, or wherever Pops is. Wherever he is, you know he's looking down on you, and shaking his head.

Von chuckles, and shakes his own head, at the thought.

Fuck it. I'm writing my name in that book. I'm claiming it. It's mine, now. My book.

I can't take it with me, because it's such a beast. But one of these days, I'll come back here, and Pastor Tom will still have it. He'll take good care of it. He'll put it to better use than I ever would, saving souls with it or whatnot.

And when I do come back, I'll buy Pastor Tom a new trailer, and he'll smile, and be like, man, it sure was a good thing I helped you, when you were down and out.

Hell, maybe I'll even buy him a new church.

Let's not get carried away. Stay in the now.

He searches the trailer for a pen. He expects Pastor Tom to

come in and check on him at some point, but there is no sign of the old coot.

He'd settle for a sharpie. A pencil, even.

A fucking crayon.

How is it this guy doesn't have anything to write with?

In the church, surely. Construction pencils.

Von cleans himself up and heads across the dusty yard to the church. The side door is open, but the church's emptiness echoes the tread and scuff of his boots back to him. The scaffolding is empty. Perhaps Pastor Tom made a run to the hardware store.

It's a shame, he thinks. *I was going to give him a hand today.*

Oh, well. His loss.

The parking lot is empty. There aren't even any cars driving by on the road out at the end of the driveway. Something about the quietness of the place spooks him. He feels like he's surrounded by a circle of spinning ghosts, holding hands, whose mouths are moving, but whose singing is inaudible. He sets off walking across the parking lot. Down the road.

It isn't till he reaches the main road that a car rushes past. And then the sweat starts trickling down his back again. Like he's back in the land of the living. He turns his face and his feet toward the sun.

Doesn't take him long, walking along Tamiami Trail, before he's questioning why he was ever in a hurry to return to this bullshit.

CHAPTER
TWENTY

HE REACHES the beach just as that big ball of fire is nearing the water. A few clouds stretch out above him, pink streaks shading to purple across a fading blue canvas.

The beach is dotted with couples and small groups that have come to watch the death of yet another day, phones out, hoping for a spectacularly gory display of bright, bloody entrails splashed across the firmament, but he can tell there aren't enough clouds in the right places for that to happen.

He kicks out of his boots, leaves them on the sand. Walks between two couples on his way to the water, before he realizes that one of the pairs is a young man and woman—he in a tie, she in a white dress—and the other a photographer and her assistant. The young man has his pants cuffed up to his knees, and they are wading in the shallows, gentle waves washing over their feet, as the photographer tries to capture them with the orange sun in the background. He and Shelly did the same thing, back in the day. Just with a selfie stick. And then the pics didn't come out the way she wanted, and they never got them printed or framed or anything like that. And now she's probably long since deleted them off her phone, and from her memory. But not from his. Not from his.

That's how it all starts, he thinks. *Wading in the shallows. Wait till they get out in the deep water, where it's sink or swim. With the sharks.*

The water is cold, then cool, then warm. The gulf waves are tentative, barely even ripples. He bends forward and scoops water into his hands, splashes it over his head, several times, then over his face, down over the scruff that has taken root along his chin in the past days. When he straightens, the water drips down his neck, onto his chest. The steady breeze unpeels his shirt from his back, billows it out behind him as he lifts his arms.

Ain't this the life, he thinks.

He watches as the sun grows even larger, even redder, until it is just a sliver at the horizon, and then gone, in a puff of green. The afterimage is almost painfully bright against the backs of his eyelids.

He turns back toward the beach, even as the couples and families and vacationers turn back toward their rentals. He retrieves his boots, and walks down the beach until he comes to a set of broken wooden pilings. He sits on the cracked concrete foundation, dusted with sand, and waits for his feet to dry before brushing them clean so he can stuff them back into his boots.

If there was ever a time for a cigarette...

He walks down the beach, near the water's edge, where the sand is packed firm. He's heading south, which is not according to plan, but he wants to retrieve his camo.

He knows he should leave it.

But he also knows—if he's being honest—that it isn't really about the camo.

It's about her. About Jasmine. Nora Lukacs.

Did she give him up? Did she tell Alvin where to find him?

Maybe he hauled her in for more questioning, but she held the line, refused to rat him out.

He comes to Delasol, Building One. Wanders up into the softer sand, where the community lounge chairs have been stacked and chained for the day. He follows a line of palms to the other side of the building. Behind a wooden fence sits the pool; a faint *whumpa-thumpa* from the tiki bar intermittently fights its way through the stiff breeze to reach his ears, as he moves along the edge of the parking lot to the far side, near the marina.

He counts the floors, until he has reached thirteen. Then over from the end, one, two, three.

A light!

And... is that even a silhouette, at the balcony? The shape of a woman?

Could it be Jasmine? Looking out at the rising moon, wondering where he is?

He crosses back over to the pool. Follows the fence to the entrance, and the directory.

N. Lukacs. Her name is still there. He keys in the code, and the door buzzes. He waves at the woman behind the desk as he heads toward the elevators.

Act like you belong.

When he reaches fourteen he hears voices, sees light spilling from Jasmine's open door into the hallway. He approaches, peers in. Several black trash bags stuffed full sit on the kitchen floor, alongside two bins on wheels, piled high with clothes. His black camo is right there! On top of the second bin. As he picks his way among the trash bags deeper into the kitchen, a grunt draws his attention into the living room, where two men are levering the armchair onto a dolly.

The man facing him, a black man, brow beaded with sweat, freezes; the man with his back to him continues leaning and lifting, and the chair only partially makes it onto the dolly, which kicks out from under and skitters into the couch. The closer man curses as he wrestles with the unbalanced, overstuffed chair.

"Who're you?" the other one demands.

He is about to turn and make his escape, when movement at the balcony door catches his eye.

Jasmine?

The bright interior and the dark exterior have made a mirror out of the sliding glass panels. A hand comes into the light, breaks that mirror illusion, reaches for the handle to draw the door open. He glimpses a bare knee, a leg, perhaps even a foot angled downward, the heel elevated.

A last glimpse—

"Hey!" the black man shouts, staggering to his feet.

Von reaches for his gear, grabs it. "This is mine," he says. And then he's out the door, heading for the stairwell, feet pounding down the hallway behind him.

"Come back!"

He hits the door and jumps down the first flight—his left foot pops and his calf seems to explode when he lands. Still he rounds the landing and skips down the next flight, left hand now gripping the railing for support.

Feet clatter and scuff on the steps above him.

"Thief!" a voice calls out. But the footfalls have stopped.

"Fuck it," he hears from above. "That bin was going in the trash anyway."

The door closes behind them with a bang that echoes down the cinderblocks.

Von strips off the shorts and print shirt, pulls on his dark camo. Laces up his boots.

Should never have come back here, he thinks.

What did you think, she was going to be waiting for you? Welcome you home with open arms?

She's just a woman, like any other.

And ain't no woman worth going to prison for.

At the bottom of the stairwell are two doors. One to the lobby, one to the outside.

He cracks open the lobby door. A sheriff is talking to the woman behind the desk; Alvin is already on his way toward the elevators. He eases the door shut and steps back.

Von pushes through the other door, despite the red-and-black *WARNING* and *PROHIBIDO* signs. Alarm bells clang while he limps across the parking lot. From there, he cuts through a small stand of trees into a clearing. A fairway of soft watered grass. He walks along the edge of the fairway, then cuts across the green. A little white flag waves at him from the hole—

Ain't that a bitch, he thinks, when he sees the number, two dark digits in the moonlight, adding up to four. He removes the flag from the cup, and drops it onto the green.

Gotta do something to change my luck.

Sirens are echoing from the road ahead of him, then turning into the Delasol parking lot behind. If he can make it to the road, and across into the residential developments there, he should be able to find a hiding place. Maybe even an empty vacation home where he can hide out for the night.

He crosses another fairway, pushes through cypresses and has hauled himself up to the top of the wall when he sees a sheriff's SUV pulled over on the shoulder, red and blue lights flashing. One of the deputies leans against the side of the vehicle, while the other smokes a cigarette, resting his foot on the wheel. Von drops down, falls back on his butt as he loses his balance on his one good leg.

He shuffles off along the wall. Through underbrush and scrub pines he comes to another fence, this one chain-link topped with a V of barbed wire. He goes for it anyway, climbing at one of the brackets. In the end he has to sort of roll his groin over it, and while the hunting pants are tough, they still snag and catch and rip on the barbs, which penetrate and jab into his skin at various points. Eventually he rolls off and flops free into a bed of pine needles on the far side, with several rips in his pants and shirt. Everything hurts—his wrist, his foot, his leg, his lacerated inner thighs and chest and arms.

Pain is our brain's way of letting us know that we must correct our course. Isn't that what Mr. Counselor Dude used to say?

Something like that.

Might not be a bad thing, he thinks, as he stands and shakes his head, *but that don't make it a good thing, either.*

He hides in the trees, catching his breath. The sirens are on all sides now, and seem to be coming closer. Tightening the noose down around his neck.

Then he sees it, through the densely clustered palmettos and scrub pines—a waving forest of white masts.

The marina.

He runs through the gate, heedless of the polo-shirted security guard who shouts behind him. His feet pound down the wooden planking. He's going to dive off the end, and swim to the mangrove swamps at the far side.

Before he can leap, though, a boat comes putt-putting into its slip. Just a modest little fishing boat, with a central tower and several rods sticking up out of tubular holders. An older guy behind the wheel, bringing it in single-handed, bored, while his wife stands at the gunwale with a loop of nylon in her hand.

The gun is out of his waistband. It's loaded, so he keeps his finger off the trigger. The sight of it should be enough. He hops on board, and barks at the lady, "Get off." He's got the gun trained on the pilot. He's gray-haired at the temples, but young, for a retiree. Wiry. He leans forward, reaching for something under the wheel.

Von strides right up to him and points the gun in his face.

"You got insurance, right?"

When the guy gives him a quizzical look, Von reaches over the low windshield and touches the barrel right to his forehead.

"Insurance!" he yells. "You got it, right?"

The guy nods. He has lifted his hands, tentatively, to shoulder height.

"Then don't be a hero, dude. Fuck off."

The guy sidles off the high chair. Von wheels back toward the woman and aims the gun in her direction, which causes her to duck and scream. "I told you to get off the boat, bitch!"

The gunwale bumps into the dock, and she scrambles over the edge. From her knees she pulls the back of the boat into the dock as well.

Von turns back to the guy, who's standing now, hands lowered. Frowning. Still weighing his chances. Von smiles as he trains the gun on his gut.

"You'll get 'er back," he says.

The sirens are close now. He can hear shouting back at the guardhouse.

Von waves the gun at him. Pulls the hammer back.

"Asshole," the man says. But he's moving. He places both hands on his bent knee, pushes himself up and out of the gently rocking boat.

As soon as the guy is standing on the dock, Von throws it into reverse. He backs away from the dock as a couple of sheriff's deputies come pounding down the boards. Von doesn't raise the gun—in fact he chucks it forward, onto the dashboard—and he ducks down.

"Shoot him!" the man urges them, and the deputies have their hands resting on their holstered weapons, but they do not remove them. He's given them no reason to fire at him. One speaks into his shoulder-slung walkie-talkie.

Von throws it into forward, and starts cruising down the inlet. The fuel gauge reads half a tank.

At least it ain't on empty, he thinks. *Finally, my luck has turned.*

The sirens are screaming off to the left, but soon they are behind him, over his shoulder. Fading. One last turn, and he'll be out into the open sea.

And from there?

Down to the Keys. Half a tank should be enough to get me all the way there.

He's humming, along with the engine. Once in the Keys, he's sure he can hook up with a construction crew. Or at least a demo crew. They don't ask so many questions on demo. No skill required, just strong backs.

He rounds the corner, plows through the gentle waves lapping into the inlet, out into the deeper waters of the gulf. He steers the craft south and really opens up the throttle, luxuriating in the freedom of movement, the roar in his ears, the rush in his face.

Maybe Raul was right, and it's only now that he's ready to hear it. Maybe he does just need some months of honest, hard work to get his life back on track. A fresh start. A new place, new people. A new identity. And then, in a few years, he'll come back with a career, and some money, and this time Tara will be able to *recognize* him, and she'll *see* him for who he is—and he'll see the pride shining in her eyes.

Maybe even Shelly will have to admit, begrudgingly, that he looks good, better than she expected him to—better than he ever has—because she'll be able to see not just the strength in his arms, but the peace on his brow. She'll be able to see, from the light in his eyes, that he's made an honest man of himself.

A boat joins him, in the darkness. A big, powerful boat. It glides up alongside him, effortlessly matching his pace. A bullhorn barks and squawks. He can't make out the words over the roar of the engines and the whipping wind, but he can imagine what they're saying. A spotlight suddenly picks him out—the glare makes it hard for him to see.

He reaches forward. From out of the mess of sunglasses and hats and tubes of sunblock and bug spray on the dash he plucks the revolver.

He's got one chance. All he needs is one clean shot, to knock out that light, so they won't be able to see him—and so he can at least see where he's going. It's the toughest shot he'll ever have to make.

Lord knows, I ain't exactly been hitting the mark since I got out.

He raises the revolver, and tries to sight down along it. Between the side-to-side, up-and-down slipping of his boat, and the erratic pitching of the other boat, it's going to take a miracle. Divine intervention.

Deep breath, and he pulls the trigger.

The light winks out.

No way! What a shot!

Luck is truly smiling on me today, finally!

Firefly flashes flicker in the darkness, and what feels like a huge fist smashes him in the chest, another in the ribs. The boat rocks and pitches him forward against the console and then back, off balance, over the gunwale and into icy water reaching into his clothes, filling his nose and his mouth, pulling him down, and down.

He swims to the surface, and now wishes he didn't have the heavy pants and long-sleeve shirt restricting his churning legs, their sodden weight dragging him downward. He strokes, and sputters—his body is bruised and battered. He is dazed, as though he struck his head.

He swims after the boat, but it is long gone, the throttle

still open. There are voices, but they are distant, and intermittent, as his head dunks underwater again.

He surfaces, splutters. Set his sights on the lights at the shore, and takes a stroke toward them—only he cannot lift his arm from the surface, it is too heavy, the sleeve weighted by the water, though there is something heavier than that, something leaden and reluctant within himself. The boots aren't helping. He tries to shove one off with the toe of the other foot, but the moment he stops kicking, his head sinks under again.

Back to the surface, he is tiring. Exhausted, even.

A tower looms up in the darkness, there, ahead of him. It is the Delasol. He is sure of it. There is a light burning in one of the upper floors—could be the thirteenth. Or the fourteenth. Three balconies from the end. He thought he'd left it behind, but it looks so familiar...

He reaches his left arm forward, tries to kick himself in that direction.

It's a shame, isn't it, he thinks. *It was all going so well there.* His laugh is choked back by a wave filling his mouth. *For a minute.*

Is that a figure, there, silhouetted against the light? A woman's figure, diminutive, short hair, hands on the railing, drawn out to the balcony by the commotion?

Is that Jasmine, looking down at me?

He thrusts his head above the water, and calls out with all his strength. "Jasmine!"

He bobs under, up again.

"Nora!"

A wave washes over him, and then another. The icy water clutches at him. These damn clothes are so heavy, but his fingers are shivering so bad that he can't undo the first button.

He reaches out toward the distant light, but his hand is invisible in the inky black. The balcony shimmers and fades, as though a cloud has passed between him and that high place.

It wasn't all that long ago that he'd been standing up there, in that tower, gazing out from the balcony. On top of the world.

He had his chance—a week's worth of chances—to experience flying.

Each time he'd turned away, so sure he would regret it on the way down. And now, turns out—his laugh turns into spluttering, again—now he'd give anything to swap places. To stand on that railing, balance for a moment, and dive down toward that pool.

Maybe a certain amount of regret is inevitable, he thinks. *No matter how you lived. Even when you go out guns blazing.*

There are voices, coming closer. A pole bounces against his arms, into his hands. He grabs ahold of it—a reflex—then pushes it away.

"Look inside your heart," Pastor Tom says. Or maybe it's Mr. Counselor Dude. "Peace can only come from within."

Von ceases his struggles. Stops kicking, and treading, and paddling. Allows his sodden weight to carry him down. He's no longer shivering, his body finally getting used to the water.

I pulled four years no problem, he thinks, as he drifts. *Ain't nothin' but a bid.*

Just another trip to the Big House.

Be out in no time...

no time at all

AFTERWORD

In writing this novel I borrowed the plot of Egyptian novelist —and 1988 Nobel Prize-winner—Naguib Mahfouz's excellent short novel from 1961, *The Thief and the Dogs*.

After reading Trevor Le Gassick's 1984 English translation, I set about outlining the story. I often do this with novels I admire, in the hopes of analyzing their effects on me as a reader and prying into their techniques, to learn from them as a writer. In the process of doing this, an American version of Mahfouz's main character, Said Mahran, began to speak up, and insert himself into the outline. The novel's various locales also began to shift, in my mind, from the shimmering desert heat of 1950s Egypt in the aftermath of the Revolution, to the sweltering tropical humidity of modern-day Southwest Florida —a time and place that has suffered its own shocks and aftershocks, natural, political, and cultural. Once the main character revealed his name to me—Von—I felt like an invitation had been extended, across cultures and across time, that I would be foolish to refuse.

So I set out to write my own version. A fan fic, unabashed. Unashamed.

Well, a little ashamed, I suppose. Hence the present florid attempt to justify my theft.

Am I no better than Von? Am I nothing more than a petty thief, who will turn to any popular mantra to justify his behavior? The old saw, "Good writers imitate; great writers steal"—is that the extent of my defense?

First of all, I am telling you this up front. Actually, it's the opposite of "up front," here in the back matter, presumably after you've already read the book, but I am fully and publicly acknowledging my debt. (I hope you do not now see me as a double thief, to have both stolen another writer's work *and* several hours of your precious time.)

Secondly, Naguib Mahfouz is brilliant. Easily one of my favorite writers, he works with an incredible range and variety of genres and styles and themes throughout his body of work. If by publishing this book, and this afterword, I can encourage even just one more western reader (or two) to seek out his works and read them—including *The Thief and the Dogs*, of course—then I shall feel absolved of any literary sins I may have committed.

Thirdly, in transposing *The Thief and the Dogs* into *Dig Two Graves*, I have expanded Mahfouz's 40,000-word very short novel into a 56,000-word short novel. Much of this increased length comes from spending more time in Von's head and perspective. Of course, longer does not mean better—often quite the opposite. The spareness of *The Thief and the Dogs* is one of the qualities I most admire about it, and a quality I tried to hew to in my version, much as the additional words belie such a claim.

Lastly, and most personally, at the outset of this plea I referred to an "invitation," and to Von "speaking up" and "revealing his name." In the past I have always rolled my eyes when authors have referred to their characters as independent people, magically appearing, "speaking" to them and having "wills of their own." This sort of intuition, or individuation, has always eluded me. Which may well explain why I have struggled with creating believable characters, and why I have not written more stories that I—as well as others in the industry—have deemed publishable. So I wanted to "open my heart," if you will, to this character, despicable as he may be, and pursue his story, with open eyes, to its bitter end. I am thankful for that experience.

As I am thankful for your patience with my justifications for my thievery. I will leave it to you to decide whether they are reasonable, or craven; noble, or petty; dignified, or brazen.

But read *The Thief and the Dogs* before rendering your verdict! You will not be disappointed. And, should you do so, while I will not have settled all of my debts—not by a long shot—I will, at least, have paid my homage in full.

Fort Myers Beach, 2025

ACKNOWLEDGMENTS

Many thanks to James Rahn and Daniel Sheinberg for their insightful criticism of the first draft.

I'm very grateful to Robin Seavill for his expert editorial eye.

Special thanks to Jake Clark for the beautiful cover design.

ABOUT THE AUTHOR

First act: raised a Mennonite in Lancaster, Pennsylvania; went to Harvard and the Escuela de Letras in Madrid with dreams of becoming a writer.

Second act: married my high school sweetheart; settled in Philadelphia; stumbled upon a career in cataloguing rare books; helped raise two fantastic children into adulthood while getting divorced along the way.

Third act: left rare books and Philadelphia behind to throw myself fully into writing, publishing, and making videos as The Aisle of Misfit Books. Visit his website for recent news: andrewhallman.com.

PREVIOUS PUBLICATIONS

AMBA: An Action-Adventure Thriller

MIRRENWOOD: A Tale of the Unicorn

Made in the USA
Las Vegas, NV
29 January 2026

40637382R00132